P9-EJY-848

LONE STAR

AND THE HORSE THIEVES

JOVE BOOKS, NEW YORK

LONE STAR AND THE HORSE THIEVES

A Jove Book / published by arrangement with
the author

PRINTING HISTORY
Jove edition / March 1992

ISBN: 0-515-10809-X

Jove Books are published by The Berkley Publishing Group,
200 Madison Avenue, New York, New York 10016.
The name "JOVE" and the "J" logo
are trademarks belonging to Jove Publications, Inc.

PRINTED IN THE UNITED STATES OF AMERICA

10 9 8 7 6 5 4 3 2 1

MISTAKEN FOR A SPY. . .

The Indians swarmed on Ki, grabbing his arms and legs to hold him motionless in spite of his struggles. Then the leader bound Ki's arms and legs with supple leather thongs and two of the warriors threw him roughly across the back of his horse. With Ki's head hanging on one side of the horse, his legs dangling on the other, and one of the Indians leading the animal, the group started moving upriver on the narrow path beside its bank . . .

* * *

This title also includes an exciting excerpt from *Journal of the Gun Years* by Richard Matheson. Ride the Wild West with Clay Halser, the fastest gun west of the Mississippi!

LONE STAR

AND THE HORSE THIEVES

★

Chapter 1

"I was quite surprised when I saw you in the dining car at noon," Jessie said. She gestured to the man with her to sit in the position nearest the window of her small stateroom on the eastbound train. "After the bank's annual board meeting we members usually go our separate ways and don't see each other for a year."

"You're no more surprised to see me than I was to see you," Clay Fuller replied. "But it seems that every year when that board meeting brings me to California I have to leave in a hurry for another meeting somewhere in the East, usually in Chicago, so I find it easier and more convenient to travel on one of the northern railroad lines. But where is the young Chinese man who attended the meeting with you? Ki, I think you called him."

"I'd imagine he's found some other Orientals among the passengers and is playing one of their gambling games with them," Jessie said. "I like to have Ki attend important meetings with me because in addition to being a shrewd judge of human nature he has a very retentive mind. He's my good right hand in managing the Starbuck holdings."

"Well, I'm very glad we're on the same train," Fuller said. "Perhaps we can talk about some of the things we've mentioned during our brief chats at those board meetings. I know you have a big ranch somewhere in Texas. It's been my idea for some time to buy a place in the West where it'll be possible to get completely away from business pressures."

"I can certainly understand that." Jessie smiled. "My Circle Star Ranch is really home to me in a way that a big-city flat or even a large house could never be. And I won't say I'm sorry not to be going to the East Coast, in spite of running into you, because I'll be getting off at our Circle Star station stop late tomorrow. If you have some time to spare, I'd be glad to have you visit my ranch."

"I'm afraid that's impossible," Fuller replied. "Though I appreciate your invitation. I've wanted to get a look at the Southwest and West for quite a while, but this is the first time I've been able to take the southern route back to the East Coast."

"It's too bad that we didn't run into one another before we got so far east," Jessie said. "You'll see a great deal of new country, if you've never taken this trip before."

"I've already learned that." Fuller nodded. "And I'm sure you could've explained some of the puzzling things I've noticed since we left Los Angeles."

"There's very little to explain about the desert country we've been traveling through, except that it doesn't have much water," Jessie said. "But we're getting close to my own home range now. You'll even be able to get a glimpse of the northern boundaries of my Circle Star Ranch, even if you don't have time to visit it."

"I wish I could stop for a visit, Jessie. But I'm sure you'll understand why I cannot."

"Of course I do," she said. "No explanations are necessary."

"You know," Fuller continued, "the very idea of having the kind of life a big ranch offers really appeals to me. But it's the same situation I run into constantly. I'm trying to keep up with a very tight schedule. I suppose that's why

2

I've gotten the idea that I'd enjoy living like a cowboy."

"I'm afraid you don't know what a rough life it can be," Jessie said. "There are times when ranching is very hard work, Clay."

From his position, Fuller could look out the window over Jessie's shoulder. He gestured toward it as he said, "You'd never know it by looking at those carefree cowboys out there."

Jessie turned to look at the line of a half-dozen riders that had just come into view. Fuller said, "Those men don't seem to have a worry in the world, even though I haven't any ideas about what cowboys are supposed to do."

Jessie leaned forward to get a better look at the horsemen, who were still some distance from the train, mounting the upslope toward the railroad tracks. She could see that there were eight mounted men in the group, which was perhaps a quarter of a mile away.

"Jessie, where do you suppose those cowboys are going?" Fuller asked. "I don't see any cattle for them to herd. It just looks to me like they're trying to beat us to the top of that rise ahead. Don't they know that a horse never will win a race with a locomotive?"

Jessie turned back to face Fuller and said soberly, "Those men aren't just racing the train for sport, Clay. They don't want to beat us to that crest up ahead. What they're trying to do is get to the train when it's slowed down near the top of the slope, because unless my guess is very wrong, they're not cowboys. They're bandits."

"Now, wait a minute, Jessie!" Clay protested. "What makes you think they're planning to hold up the train? How do you know they're not some of your western field hands?"

"For one thing, they're all carrying rifles across their saddle horns, ready to use," she told him. Her voice was as calmly unworried as it might have been if she were inviting Clay to dinner. "Cowboys don't ride that way unless there's trouble coming up."

3

"And that's the only reason you've got for calling them bandits?"

"It's reason enough," Jessie replied. "Cowhands carry rifles in their saddle scabbards and don't take them out until they're about to use them. Besides, I've run into more than one bunch of outlaws. And I'd be very much surprised if holding up this train isn't just exactly what those men have in mind."

As Jessie spoke she was getting to her feet. She lifted her small crocodile-skin valise from the luggage rack and opened it. Reaching into the bag, she brought out her Colt in its tooled leather holster. Fuller watched her, his eyes opening wide in surprise when he saw the revolver.

"Do you carry that gun with you wherever you go?" he asked.

"Of course," Jessie answered. "I always wear a gunbelt and carry a rifle when I'm riding the range on the Circle Star, and habits are hard to break. Besides that, I've learned that men use guns in your big civilized cities about as often as cowhands do on the range."

She stepped to the window to get a better look at the riders. The train was starting up the long grade now, slowing almost imperceptibly. By this time the band of horsemen had closed the gap until less than a quarter of a mile separated them from the locomotive. Four of the men were galloping straight toward the tracks. Their companions were breaking up their clustered formation now, reining their horses to form a roughly spaced line stretching from the engine to the observation coach.

Suddenly the man in the lead of the riders reined his mount toward the locomotive. He raised his rifle as he turned his horse. Without shouldering the weapon, handling it like a pistol, he fired a shot at the puffing locomotive. The metallic ringing of the bullet landing somewhere on the engine was loud and sharper than the squeals of the train's wheels rasping on the rails.

"He's shooting at us!" Clay exclaimed.

"Of course." Jessie's voice was calm. "But he's not as

4

interested in us as he is in trying to get the engineer to stop the train."

As though her words had been a cue, the squeals of steel wheels skidding on steel rails cut through the lesser noises and the train began to slow down.

Jessie waited until the coach stopped swaying after it had come to a halt. Then she stepped up to the window and swung the butt of her Colt against the pane. The glass shattered into shards with a tinkling noise. Dropping to her knees in front of the window, she leaned forward and raised her head until she could peer out. At the front of the train she saw one of the outlaws, still in the saddle, his rifle shouldered now, covering the engine crew.

Taking quick aim at the outlaw leader, Jessie squeezed off a shot. The mounted man jerked in his saddle, his head snapping back, his arms drooping. His wide-brimmed hat fell away as his head moved, and while he was still shifting the rifle, his arms dropped. He slumped forward, his arms drooping now and his neck limp. For a moment he hung poised on the shoulders of his horse before toppling to the ground.

"You . . . you shot him!" Clay exclaimed.

"Of course. But he shot first," she replied calmly.

Jessie had not taken her eyes from the window while she was speaking. She kept shifting her gaze from one to another of the attackers, looking for one close enough to the coach for her pistol fire to be effective. Before she'd found a target, the sharp crack of several of the rifles broke the air and bullets thunked into the side of the coach below the window where Jessie and Clay were poised.

By this time single shots were sounding from the other outlaws, and these were echoed now and again by the fainter sounds of shooting from the opposite side of the coaches. On the side where Jessie and Clay Fuller were located the renegade crew of attackers was closer to the train. Now a few scattered rounds were beginning to come from the train, as the passengers who carried weapons joined in firing through

5

the coach windows at the horsemen.

When Jessie began turning her head from side to side, looking for a fresh target, she saw another of the attackers slump in his saddle as a slug took him. The horse ridden by another of the outlaws had obviously been hit by the men firing from the train. It was bucking and twirling, and its gyrations soon threw its rider from the saddle. The man who'd fallen leaped to his feet and scrabbled toward his limping horse, but the panicked beast was zigzagging across the prairie now and eluded him.

Then a shout sounded from one of the outlaws near the rear of the group. His companions reined their mounts around and began spurring away from the tracks. A shot or two still came from the train now and then, the slugs kicking up prairie dust, but these died away quickly as the would-be holdup men continued to retreat.

Jessie had not risen from her kneeling position beside the shattered window. All her attention was concentrated on the fleeing frustrated outlaws as their figures grew smaller in the distance. She started to stand up. Fuller took her arm and helped her. For a moment neither of them spoke.

"Does this sort of thing happen all the time in this part of the country?" he asked.

Jessie shook her head. "It used to be pretty constant, especially in stretches like this where there's a long upgrade to slow the train down. By now, though, the outlaws who specialized in robbing trains have pretty much learned that it's not as easy as it was before the railroads began putting rifles on the trains and telling their crews to use them. Why, I can't remember having read about a train robbery for months."

"Well, this is my first experience with one," Fuller confessed. "And I'm a bit surprised as well as pleased that the shooting didn't bother me. I noticed that you took it in stride, too."

"I've been—" Jessie began, but broke off as the door of the little stateroom opened and Ki stepped inside.

"You're all right, Jessie?" he asked.

6

"Certainly," she replied. "I don't suppose you could do anything but watch?"

"None of that bunch ever got close enough for me to reach with a *shuriken*," Ki told her. "And the coach was so crowded, with the passengers milling around in the aisle, that I didn't even try to get close to one of the vestibules."

"You've seen Ki, but you've never really met him before," Jessie said as she turned to Fuller. "Bare-bones introductions at board meetings don't count. This is Ki, my good right arm. As I told you a moment ago, he looks after things on the Circle Star when I'm busy with other matters."

"I'm very happy to meet you, Ki," Fuller replied. "But who looks after your ranch when both of you are away?"

"Oh, I have a very competent foreman," Jessie said. "And right now there's very little to be done on my ranch. Our busy time at the Circle Star doesn't start until we start cutting out steers for the market herd."

"And you took—" Fuller began, but stopped short as a cursory rapping rattled from the door.

It opened as the conductor stuck his head into the state-room, glanced around, and asked, "Any of you folks get hurt?"

"All of us are in good shape," Jessie replied. "I hope all the other passengers are, too."

"Nobody got shot, as far as I've found out up till now," the conductor replied. "And I'm sure not going to stop the train until we get to a place where those robbers can't catch up with us. But I see you got a busted window. I'll get one of the baggage hands to put some boards over it soon as we get to moving again. We won't—" A long, quivering toot from the locomotive whistle sounded, interrupting the conductor before he'd finished. He paused, then went on, "That's the engineer wanting to know why I haven't given him the highball yet. I better get busy, because we'll be running late all up the line if we don't get started real quick."

As the conductor turned to leave, Ki said, "I think it might be wise for me to move, too, back to my regular seat. For

7

all we know, those outlaws might get over their panic and decide to come back for another try."

"I doubt that they'll do that." Jessie frowned.

"I suppose it is an outside possibility, though," Fuller put in.

"Anything's possible, of course," Jessie agreed. She turned to Ki and went on, "Do what you think is necessary, Ki. Clay and I will finish our chat, which the outlaws interrupted."

She'd barely finished speaking when two long blasts from the locomotive sounded. Even before their echoes had died away the sharp metallic bangs of coach couplings began clattering through the glassless window. The coach lurched and then began moving slowly ahead.

Gesturing toward the green plush-upholstered seat, Jessie suggested, "We might as well make ourselves as comfortable as possible."

At the same time both she and Fuller turned toward the seat. Somehow their arms and feet got entangled. Jessie would have fallen if Fuller had not caught her and wrapped his arms around her.

Instinctively, Jessie twisted her torso while she was still held in Fuller's arms. The rough tweeded fabric of his Scotch wool jacket pressing against her thin blouse rasped softly across her full breasts and a little shiver rippled through Jessie's body before he released her from his firm embrace. At last he let his arms drop, but held her hand while she completed her turn and regained her seat.

"I'm sorry that I grabbed you the way I did," Fuller told her. "I hope I didn't hold you too tightly while I was trying to help you."

"Of course not," Jessie replied. She was silent for a moment, then went on, "I appreciated your thoughtfulness." When Fuller said nothing, she added, "Would it surprise you if I told you that I enjoyed being in your arms as much as you seemed to enjoy holding me?"

Fuller gazed at her, his eyes widening. He saw a smile forming on Jessie's full lips and asked her, "You're sure?"

"I seldom say anything I'm not sure of," she replied. "And if you want proof—" Breaking off her conversation, Jessie stepped closer to him and tilted her head back.

Fuller hesitated for only a moment before bending forward to find her lips with his, but Jessie did not hesitate once their caress was joined. She slipped the tip of her tongue forward, and this time Fuller's response came without hesitation. He met her tongue with his, and their clinging embrace went on and on until a rapping sounded on the stateroom door. They dropped their arms and parted hastily.

"It's the man with the cover for the broken window," Jessie said as she stepped to the door and opened it.

A man wearing a railroad cap and overalls stood in the aisle. He asked, "You the lady with the busted window?"

"Yes," Jessie replied. "And I can see that you're the man who's come to fix it."

"That's right," he agreed. "It's just going to take me a few minutes, but I got to have working room, so if you don't mind—"

Fuller spoke up quickly, "Suppose we go to the dining car, Jessie. I'm sure they've started serving by this time. We'll have an early dinner and perhaps a drink in the club car or—"

"That's a very good idea." Jessie nodded. She locked Fuller's eyes with hers as she went on, "And I'm sure we'll find something to keep us from getting bored afterwards."

For several minutes Clay Fuller had been silent, lying propped on an elbow beside Jessie on the narrow bed of her stateroom. Jessie reached a hand up to caress his face. She drew a finger down his forehead to his nose, ran the fingertip along the contours of his cleft chin, and then brushed it lightly along his lips.

"Would you take the usual penny for your thoughts?" she asked.

"Even less," he replied. "I'm just regretting that in all the times we've been together at those bank board meetings I've never asked you to dinner or talked with you in anything but the usual platitudes."

Jessie smiled, her eyes veiled with satisfaction as she asked, "But now that you've broken the ice?"

"I'll never be able to be with you long enough," he replied.

"That's a very nice compliment, Clay," Jessie replied. "But—"

"No buts!" he broke in. "Ever since we've been in this little stateroom so close together, even before that, when we were just standing chatting in the dining car, all that I've been able to think about is holding you and kissing you, and I could hardly force myself to let go of you—"

"You know I wouldn't try to stop you from holding me now," she suggested. "And if that might lead to something else—"

Clay did not wait for her to finish. He bent to find her lips with his, and as their tongues entwined, her hands moved to his groin. Under her expert caresses, he swelled and stiffened.

When she could feel his readiness, Jessie shifted as best she could in the narrow Pullman berth while Clay moved to lift himself above her. She sprawled her thighs while she guided him, and Clay wasted no time, but thrust lustily in a single hard lunge that brought a gasp of pleasure to her lips and a twist to her supple hips.

Now Jessie locked her legs around her lover's back and matched his deep penetrations with upward gyrations of her hips that brought their bodies together with a soft thwacking. Their rhythmic pleasuring went on and on until tremors were sweeping through Jessie's agile form and Clay was beginning to pant stertorously.

"Stop and just hold yourself in me, Clay," Jessie gasped. "We don't want this to end too soon."

Buried in her, Clay stopped stroking until Jessie's quivering subsided. They lay quietly motionless for a moment or two longer; then Jessie raised her hips and began wriggling them from side to side as a signal to her lover. Clay resumed his stroking, and Jessie responded with vigor until once again she felt the ripples beginning to sweep through her body.

This time Clay needed neither signal nor instructions. At the conclusion of another deep penetration he pressed himself against her quivering form and lay quietly, without moving. Jessie allowed herself to relax until the small quivers of her body had stopped for several moments; then she lifted her hips to signal her lover to begin thrusting again.

Clay responded at once, but both of them had waited overlong. All too soon Jessie sensed that her lover's rhythm was becoming ragged, and now she made no further effort to delay the climax of their mutual pleasure. Instead, she began twisting her hips as she brought them up to match each of Clay's strokes.

When he felt Jessie's changing rhythm, Clay drove even faster. Then as her body tensed and a cry of pleasure burst from her lips, he drove to their mutual completion.

For a few breathless moments they lay motionless; then Jessie sighed and whispered, "You're a marvelous lover, Clay. But we both need to rest longer than we did before."

"I just don't want to leave you, Jessie," Clay protested.

"You don't have to, not yet," she answered. "Both of us know the night's been too short, and we know there can't be another like it before we have to say good-bye. If we sleep a little while now, there'll still be enough time before the train gets to the Circle Star to say our real good-bye."

★

Chapter 2

With a sigh of relief, Jessie refolded the letter she'd just finished reading and laid it on top of the stack of mail that had accumulated during her absence from the Circle Star. She turned to look at Ki. He was seated across the room, at the battered rolltop desk that had belonged to Alex, sorting the fat manila envelopes that held monthly reports of the various Starbuck enterprises. These covered many fields: banking, finance, mining, lumbering, shipping, as well as a few smaller ventures. Though most of the Starbuck business interests were located in the West, a few such as banking, stockbrokerage, and real estate, had offices in some of the large eastern cities.

"I hope you're not planning to open any of those reports tonight," Jessie told Ki. "We've done nothing but desk work during the three days we've been at home, and I'd really enjoy just going to bed soon."

"I think we both need to rest for a day or so," he replied. "And most of these reports are pretty much routine."

"Good." She nodded. "Because I've been thinking of something that we really ought to do tomorrow. Cliff Peake says those new calf pastures have been fenced, and I'm thinking of getting up early to ride out and see how the yearlings are doing on their new grazing areas."

"Will Cliff be going with us?"

"He may want to go along, but I haven't talked to him yet. He'd certainly be welcome to go with us if he wants to."

"Cliff's a good foreman," Ki said. "You never have to worry about him doing his job right. And I'm sure you'll be glad to have a chance to ride Sun again."

"Of course I will." Jessie smiled as she thought of her magnificent palomino, the horse she favored above all others. "Why don't you come along, Ki? As long as there doesn't seem to be anything in the mail that needs immediate attention, you might as well ride out to the new range with us."

"Yes, I think I need a breath of fresh air, too," Ki replied. "And so far all this mail I've been looking at is nothing but routine reports. There are only three or four letters, and you can read them anytime you get around to it."

"Which may not be for another day or two." Jessie nodded. "We've both done enough for this evening, and I'm ready to go to bed. But I'd really like a cup of hot tea first."

"I'll fix a cup for each of us," Ki volunteered. "Do you have any preference, Jessie?"

"Some of the new *Lapsang-Souchang* would really be a treat."

"Then that's what I'll brew," Ki told her.

He started across the room toward the tall, ornately gilded cabinet that had been one of Alex Starbuck's proudest possessions. It was one of many objects in the room that Jessie cherished because they carried so many memories of her dead father, whom she'd adored.

After her mother had died in giving birth to Jessie, Alex had made his only child the center of his life. Even though his meteoric career demanded and got his close attention, Alex had put business in second place whenever necessary to see that Jessie received the kind of care and education that would enable her to supervise the many successful enterprises that had made him one of America's richest and most respected men.

During much of Jessie's childhood Alex was busy fighting a sinister, vicious European cartel. The cartel's plan had been to buy or steal the key industries and financial institutions of the United States and divert America's wealth to a decadent European group. Alex's fight ended in tragedy when the cartel's hired assassination squad brought him down with a hail of bullets in a surprise attack.

As might have been expected, Jessie was greatly saddened by her beloved father's death. Then when Ki disclosed to her the details of the fight Alex had been carrying on, she resolved to pick up the battle her father had begun and carry it to a finish. After a long struggle, she finally achieved Alex's goal. The cartel and its sinister masters were totally defeated, and the threat to American freedom and prosperity was abolished.

Freed at last from the burden she'd assumed, Jessie could then begin to give all her attention to the rich heritage left her by Alex Starbuck. She proved quickly that she'd inherited her father's business acumen as well as his courage. Under her management, the wealth left her by her father multiplied and enabled her to give many struggling businesses the help they needed to grow and prosper.

Of all the bequests left by Alex, the vast Circle Star Ranch in the far western plains of Texas was the one she cherished most. The sprawling adobe main house and the rippling prairie surrounding it became her home and refuge from the grime and strife of cities. Now, as she watched Ki pouring boiling water over the fragrant *Lapsang-Souchang* tea in the teapot, Jessie relaxed in the big leather-upholstered easy chair that had been her father's.

Almost as soon as Jessie settled down, she felt the weariness of her long, jolting train trip fading away. Then her pleasant mood was broken by a pounding at the front door, echoing down the hallway.

15

"It's awfully late for visitors, and I'm certainly not expecting any." Jessie frowned.

"Could it be Cliff?" Ki asked. "Something may have happened out on the range that he's just heard about."

Jessie shook her head. "Cliff would have knocked the way he always does, three times three taps."

"But he may have sent one of the hands with a message," Ki suggested.

They'd reached the door now. Ki stepped between Jessie and the thick wooden door, lifted the night latch, and swung it open. Both he and Jessie were so surprised to see a thick swirling of white snowflakes drifting down through the night's deep shadows that for a moment or two they paid no attention to the man who stood in the doorway.

"Ain't you and Ki even going to say hello to me, Miss Jessie?" the visitor asked when she and Ki continued to gaze past him, looking at the big white flakes that scintillated against the blackness beyond the light of the open door. "Maybe you just don't remember me because it's been a while since I pulled down my pay and left here."

"Of course we remember you, Bruce!" Jessie replied, turning her attention to the unexpected visitor. "It's just that we see snow here so seldom that I couldn't take my eyes off it. I still don't quite believe what we're looking at."

"I'll say this, Jessie," Bruce told her. "You can count yourself lucky that you don't see this kind of a snow more'n once in a blue moon. I know that for sure. I've been trying to keep in front of this blasted storm since just before sundown and I'll guarantee you that it's going to get worse before it gets better."

"Well, come in out of the cold, Bruce," Jessie said. "But it might not be much better indoors after the storm gets really bad. We don't have a fire going, because until now it's been warm inside."

After their visitor had stepped into the entry hall and brushed away the big snowflakes that lay thickly on his shoulders and thighs, he turned to Jessie and said, "I know

I ain't the foreman here anymore, Miss Jessie. And I ain't trying to butt into your business. But if I was you, I'd turn out every man you got on the Circle Star and start 'em riding fence. This is setting out to be a real bad storm."

"You said you've been in it since sundown?" Ki asked. His usually calm face wore a frown now.

"Well, I seen the big black clouds up to the north of me before the sun was gone, but the snow didn't catch up to me till the wind pushed the clouds right over my head. That was just a little while after dark," Bruce replied.

"And you've been riding through this snow ever since?" Jessie asked.

"I sure 'nuff have, Miss Jessie," he replied. "First off when I noticed them clouds, I figured they'd just be carrying a gully-busting rain, but all of a sudden a little bit later that cold wind hit me and right after that the air was just full of snow."

"How far were you from the Circle Star when the snow began?" Jessie asked.

"About a half-mile the other side of the railroad," Bruce assured her. "But I'd already begun pushing my horse right hard soon as I seen the first snowflakes. You know how this kind of weather is, Miss Jessie."

"I certainly do!" Jessie replied. "We don't get snow here very often, but once in a blue moon one of these stray blizzards hits us." She turned to Ki and went on, "You'd better have Cliff turn out the hands, Ki. The range steers will have to be kept in tight herds all night, or we'll lose a lot of them."

"Of course," Ki replied. "And I'm sure you intend for us to go along and help them."

"Why, certainly!" Jessie exclaimed. "They'll need our help as badly as we need theirs! And while you're doing that, I'll go across to the cookshack and rouse Spud. Those men might be scattered out on the range for quite a while, and we've got to be sure they'll have saddle rations. So will we, for that matter. I'll tell Spud to be sure to make

17

up enough packets to go around."

Bruce said quickly, "Put my name on one of them packets, Miss Jessie. If you've got a fresh horse for me and don't mind me going with your regular hands, I'll be proud to ride with your outfit again, at least till this storm blows past."

"Now, Bruce, I'm sure you're tired from your trip—" Jessie began, but he raised a hand to stop her.

"Maybe I'm a mite tired," he admitted. "But I ain't forgot the help you gave me when I wanted to set up on my own. Besides, I know if you and Ki was at my spread and seen I needed a little bit of help, you'd be the first to give it to me."

"I'm not going to argue," Jessie said. "Because if this is as bad a storm as you say, we're certainly going to need all the help we can get. Now, there's no use for us wasting time. We'd better be getting ready for what's ahead."

Across the rolling prairie the white covering of snow threw back the rays of the rising sun. Jessie blinked in the unaccustomed brilliance as she watched Ki approach. He reached the spot where she'd reined in and pulled up beside her.

"How many downed steers did you find, Ki?" she asked.

"Not anywhere as many as I was afraid I would, Jessie. I may have missed seeing one or two in the dark, but I only found four steers that were in trouble, and after I'd gotten them on their feet and started them moving, I could see that they came through the storm in good shape. I don't think we'll lose any of those I saw. Did you run across many?"

"Two. And I only had to chouse them a little bit to get them up and get them to the nearest herd."

"Then perhaps the snow's not going to hurt us as badly as we were afraid it would," Ki suggested.

"It looks that way now, but I'm not going to get my hopes too high until we've found out what the hands ran into."

Ki nodded as he replied, "We'll know that before bedtime tonight. This storm's not like the last one we had three years ago. We didn't get the men out on the range as quick as we did this time, but we still didn't lose more than a half-dozen steers."

"I remember quite well," Jessie said. "And I hope it'll be three times three years before we get another one. But as far as I can see, our men have things pretty well in hand. The snow's already beginning to melt, so I don't think we really have too much to worry about."

"You're ready to go back to the main house, then?"

"Of course not! We'll circle around from one section to another, and see if any of the hands need help."

"I had a pretty good idea that's what you were going to say." Ki smiled. "And the odds are good that we'll find a stray or two that's been overlooked in the dark. I'm ready to start moving whenever you say the word."

Moving slowly, letting their horses pick their own footing on the treacherously slick ground, Jessie and Ki moved ahead. The sudden snow had covered the Circle Star range thoroughly, but the tops of the fence posts that marked the line and section boundaries gave them a foolproof guide. As the sun rose higher and its warmth started the snow to melting faster, their going became easier.

Two or three times Jessie and Ki got distant glimpses of the ranch hands carrying out the same job they were doing. On both occasions they exchanged waves with the distant riders. Only twice did they encounter bogged-down steers. Both the animals were yearlings, unaccustomed to being away from the shelter of a herd. The young steers were having trouble with their hooves sliding and toppling them on the film of crystallized snow that was now forming on the earth as the sun's rays began to melt the white coating. Ki was quick to dismount and give the troubled animals a boost, and once the young steers had gained their feet again they had no trouble picking their way across the range.

By the time the sun had climbed high, the dark patches of open ground had begun to outnumber those that were still covered by the thin icy film of melting snow. Jessie reined Sun to a halt, and Ki pulled up at her side as she stood up in her stirrups and gazed across the prairie.

"I think the trouble's over now, Ki," she said. "And if I know Hank, he'll be having the hands doing the same sort of checking-up that's kept us out this long."

"I'm sure you're right," Ki agreed. "What's left of the snow's melting fast, and except where it's piled up against the drift fence, it'll be gone by the middle of the afternoon."

"We might as well head back to the main house," Jessie suggested. She settled back into her saddle as she went on, "I don't mind admitting that I'm hungry, and I know the sort of meal that'll be waiting for us."

Reining around, they nudged their horses toward the heart of the Circle Star. The sun was warm on their backs, and they could see patches of winter-yellowed grass and areas of dark soil where only a short time earlier the ground had been hidden by snow.

They reached the point where they could see the ranch buildings, the work sheds and storage sheds, the corrals and bunkhouse, the mess hall with its cookshack sticking out behind it like a misplaced thumb, the big barns at the edge of the horse corrals and the imposing two-story main house. There were three or four horses at the hitch rail in front of the mess hall.

"Some of the hands who were working closest must've already covered their range and come in to eat," Ki remarked. "I don't see Cliff's horse, though, so he's probably still out checking up on the men furthest from here."

"That's one thing I'll give Cliff credit for," Jessie said. "I never feel that I have to check up on him. No matter what the job is, he stays with it until it's finished."

"I can't argue about that," Ki agreed. "He's the best foreman we've had since Bruce left to strike out on his own."

"It was certainly thoughtful of him to join in and help us," she went on. "And I'm quite curious to find out why he's showed up so suddenly."

"We're not going to have long to wait," Ki replied. "That's Bruce coming out of the mess hall now." He hesitated for a moment, and added, "I'm sure he's finished the job he volunteered to do. He must have something important that he wants to talk to you about, or he wouldn't've come here. Why don't you just ask him to go over to the main house with you? I'll get our meal and bring it over there."

"A good idea," Jessie agreed. "You know how it seems to embarrass some of the hands when I eat at the mess hall."

"Yes, there are a lot of them who get nervous anytime the boss is around. You go ahead, then, Jessie. I'll be along as soon as Cookie can dish up our food."

Entering the main house, Jessie went back to the study and cleared away the mail from the small table that stood near the easy chair she favored. She was just turning away from the desk where she'd deposited the mail when a tapping sounded at the study door. As she'd expected, when she turned, she saw Bruce Lewis standing in the open doorway, his hat in his hand.

"Your door was open, so I figured you'd expect me to come on in," he told her. "Ki said you'd have a few minutes for us to talk, Miss Jessie. So if you have . . ." His voice trailed off on a questioning note.

"I'm sorry it's taken so long for us to get around to it, Bruce," she replied to his unfinished question. "If you don't mind talking while I'm eating, I'd really like to hear whatever it is you came to talk about. I'm sure it's important, or you wouldn't've ridden all the way from your place to the Circle Star."

"It might not sound important to you," Bruce said. "But it sure is to me."

"Sit down, then," Jessie said. She gestured toward the chair that sat near the one she was heading for. "I suppose Ki told you he was bringing some food over here from the cookshack, and I certainly won't let my meal interfere with listening."

21

"You want I should start right off, or wait for Ki?" Bruce asked as they settled into their chairs. "I remember that when I was foreman here you always liked for him to know all about what was going on."

"Things haven't changed a bit." Jessie smiled. "I still think it's important for Ki to know everything that's happening on the Circle Star. But if you want to start right now, I'm sure that he can catch up with anything you might tell me before he gets here. But let me guess before you begin. I'd imagine that whatever you've got in mind has something to do with your horse ranch."

"You sure hit that with your first shot." Bruce nodded. "And I—" He broke off as Ki came in, carrying a large platter in each hand. Then he said, "Now, I won't hold you back from your vittles, Miss Jessie. If you're as starved as I was when I got back here after chousing all them steers around, you better have your breakfast or whatever it is without me bothering you with my chatter."

"I've learned to eat and listen at the same time," Jessie said assuringly. "You go right ahead, Bruce. If there's anything I don't understand, I'll stop you and ask you some questions."

"Whatever you say, then," he nodded. He settled back into the chair Jessie had indicated, shifted around for a moment, and shuffled his booted feet a bit to get comfortably seated. Then he said, "You know I been working like a plantation hand to get my little horse ranch up in Nevada Territory to where it's paying off, I guess?"

"I'm sure you must've been, just from reading that letter you wrote when you sent me the money to pay off the loan I made you to help you get started," Jessie replied. "Are you having a bad time now?"

"Oh, it's bad, all right," Bruce replied. "But not on account of I've slacked off working, or anything like that. My little spread's just beginning to pay off. But now there's a bunch of outlaws set on taking it away from me."

22

"Isn't there a sheriff or a marshal in a town close by that you can set on them?" Jessie frowned.

"Nevada Territory's not like the rest of the country, Miss Jessie. Law officers are few and far apart. Now, everything I got is in that horse ranch, and there's ten or twelve of them to just one of me. I know you don't owe me a thing, and I'm a lot more'n half-ashamed to come asking you. But if you'd be of a mind to give me a little bit of help, I'd sure be the most thankful man on God's green earth."

★

Chapter 3

Jessie did not act on the impulse that popped into her mind immediately after hearing Bruce's request. She had no doubt that he badly needed someone to lend him a hand, but at the same time she was also well aware of her own responsibility to keep her guiding hands on the many companies that made up the Starbuck commercial and industrial empire.

These had been her father's legacy, and she could not neglect it. Jessie was keenly aware that she had the responsibility to keep its banks and brokerage offices, its mines and mills and factories functioning. Without a firm guiding hand, the jobs of hundreds of people employed by the far-flung Starbuck enterprises would be in danger.

For a moment Jessie sat silent while her mind juggled the requirements on her time during the days ahead. At the same moment she was remembering all the hard work that Bruce had done when he'd been foreman on the Circle Star. He'd not only carried out his tasks willingly and efficiently, but shown unquestioning loyalty during the years he'd spent there.

Her hesitation lasted for only a few moments; then she said, "If you hadn't been pretty sure I'd help you, I don't think you'd have come here."

"Well, I got to admit you was the first one I thought about when I seen I'd bit off more'n I could chew," Bruce replied a bit sheepishly. "But I didn't feel real certain it'd even be right for me to come asking you to help me. I kept reminding myself I'm a grown-up man that oughta be able to take care of hisself, but that don't mean I wasn't doing an awful lot of hoping."

"Suppose you tell me what's been happening," Jessie suggested. "I'd also like to know more about the place in Nevada Territory where your ranch is located. I know it's somewhere along the Colorado River, but I'm not sure exactly where."

"Well, my little spread ain't the kind of place you'd call no Garden of Eden like's in the Good Book, Miss Jessie, but I'm right proud of it. It's on a great big spread of high mesa land that's got a lot of real nice stands of good grass on it, but there's another part along one side where it's sorta raw and broke-up. That's where the drop-off is to a crick bigger than lots of rivers in that dry part of the country."

When Bruce paused to take a breath, Jessie said, "I've crossed that part of Nevada Territory a time or two. It's always seemed pretty dry to me. What about water? Do you have enough?"

"Enough and some to spare, Miss Jessie. There's a little crick running through my claim close to where I built my house and barn and corrals. I dug me a well first off, but I tell you, it was really a job to push it down deep enough to strike water. Then I hit it lucky. The spring I got down to wasn't more'n about two hand-spans wide, but the water's sweet, not alkalai like so many of them places are. And so far it ain't dried up even in the middle of a hot summer."

"You're sure your claim title's clear?" she asked. "There hasn't been anybody who filed on it before?"

"Nary a soul," Bruce assured her. "Except that a while back when that territory was opening up there was a lot of land claims that got filed on, but never got proved. Them outlaws are trying to take all that land now, but they don't

26

have a smidgen of right to it. You'll recall that I been on my claim going on for two years now. The law says that in another year what I've claimed on will be mine to keep, even if somebody'd filed on it before I did."

Ki had been listening in silence. Now he spoke up. "Bruce is right about that, Jessie," he said. "When Alex was beginning to work his silver mine in Nevada Territory he ran into some old claims that had been abandoned. Of course, Alex had the money to buy them outright instead of living on them the way Bruce is having to do to keep his title. I'd be the first to agree with him if he says the outlaws he's talking about are trying to make a grab for his horse ranch."

"That's exactly what they're doing!" Bruce exclaimed. "And there's a lot more of them than me and Charley!"

"How many are in the bunch that's threatening you?" Jessie asked.

"I can't say for sure," Bruce answered, his brow puckering as he spoke. "They mostly ride in threes, but sometimes there's as many as five. And they acted pretty good the first time they made me an offer to buy me out. I told 'em no, a-course, but they come back a while later and tried again. They boosted the ante a little bit that second time, and then when I still told 'em I wasn't going to sell out they got downright mean."

"And I gather that you didn't back down?" Jessie asked.

"Not one smidgen!" Bruce answered. "I'd made up my mind I wasn't going to let 'em bluff me out of it. The trouble is that just me and my helper can't stand up very long against a bunch like that outlaw outfit, if they get real mean."

"Would a loan help you?" Jessie asked. "Couldn't you just pay out the balance you owe, instead of occupying the claim long enough to prove your title?"

Bruce shook his head. "From what I gather, the law today's been changed from the way it was when your daddy was busy there. The way that Nevada Territory homestead law reads now, if I'd had the ready money, I could've bought the land outright before I moved in on it. But the catch is that once a fellow starts living on his claimed land to prove his title, the law says he can't change and just pay it out."

"That's a very stupid law, in my book," Jessie said. "But I'm sure that it would take a long time to change it." She paused again, then nodded her head and went on. "All right, Bruce. Give Ki and me a day or so to catch up with the few things that need to be done here on the Circle Star; then we'll go to Nevada with you and see what can be done."

"Well, I must say that anyone who calls that little path up this side of the river a trail certainly needs to have a lot of imagination," Jessie remarked.

She swung off her horse and stepped to the edge of the drop-off. There, she looked down the precipitous walls of almost solid rock that formed the canyon's sides, studying the rough zigzag path they'd struggled over while mounting the steep rocky wall. Then she followed with her eyes the white-frothed surface of the river that ran along its bottom.

Jessie's view was limited to a mile or so in either direction, for here the canyon made a wide bend. Along the stretch of the canyon she could see, only the rugged massed stone formations gave a hint of the difficulties they had encountered on either side of the trail by which they'd ascended.

She spent a moment or two scanning the big crevasse. It was much deeper than it had appeared to be at a glance. Its raw stone sides bore the jagged splits and cracks of age. Some of these fractures on its walls were wide enough and deep enough to have accumulated a layer of dirt on their bottoms, and in these there were thin strands of grass growing. Rising from a few were the stunted trunks of small trees. With a final glance at the canyon bottom, Jessie shook her head and turned back to her companions.

"I can certainly see why you don't travel south or east very often, Bruce," she said. "And I can understand why the Indian Bureau would put a tribe of hostiles in this kind of country. If trouble started, it certainly wouldn't take many soldiers to keep them bottled up. Why, along those ridges up there a handful of soldiers could hold off an army of Indians. And this trail down into the canyon is rough and bad enough to make anybody think twice about crossing it."

"Well, it's a lot easier for a horse to make it up on this trail than it is for one to come up on most of the others around here," Bruce said as he stepped up beside her. "The way I've heard it is that the legislature up in Reno don't want to make it too easy for the Paiutes to get out of this canyon."

"Paiutes?" Ki frowned. "Is there an Indian reservation further up the canyon, along the river?"

"There sure is," Bruce replied. "From what I've heard, there's two or three tribes of 'em. Mostly the Paiutes are friendly, not that there's a lot of them left. The Indian Bureau brought a bunch of Chiricahuas from back east a ways. They're the real mean ones. The only Paiutes left are the ones that were still alive after they stopped fighting our cavalry."

"But do they stay on the reservation, or do they come down to your place and bother you?" Jessie asked.

"Mostly they stay where they're supposed to," Bruce replied. "It's a right big reservation, too. The valley sorta opens up a ways upriver. And from what I've heard, it seems like after the big fracas at Wounded Knee, the Indian Bureau took to putting the hostile tribes on big reservations in places where it'd be easier for the bureau's agents to ride herd on the redskins and harder for the Indians to bust out of."

"But the Paiutes aren't still hostile, are they?" Ki asked.

"Well, Ki, I don't mix with the redskins much. They stay on the reservation and I keep off of it as much as I can. But from what I've been told, they ain't as bad as they used to be," Bruce answered. "And they've been real good about letting me alone. I'd a sight rather have them for neighbors than that bunch of outlaws on the other side of my little spread."

"And there aren't any law officers close by," Jessie said again.

"Not as many as I'd like to see," Bruce told her. "But there's not many towns around here, Miss Jessie. Now and again when I ride almost all day just to get to town and buy grub, and don't see a human soul on the way there or back, I feel like I'm trying to carry a real heavy load up a pretty steep hill. I guess that's one reason why I felt like I had to go running to you and ask for help. There just wasn't anybody else I could take my troubles to."

"I'm glad you did," Jessie assured him. "If somebody who's done a good job for me needs a hand, I'm certainly not going to push them away."

"Well, I know I appreciate it," Bruce said. "But if we're going to get to my little place before the day's over, we'd better be moving along. It's an easy ride from here, mostly pretty level grassland, and we won't have to push the horses too hard to make it there before dark."

"We know about your Indian neighbors now," Jessie said to Bruce as they started off. "And about the outlaw gang that's trying to buy you out or run you off. Where *is* the nearest town?

"Navajo Spring," Bruce said. "It's only a two days' ride from where my land starts, but it's right new. It ain't such a much, maybe six houses and a store where you can buy airtights and cornmeal and flour and sugar and such-like. The biggest place that's close is Cedar City. It's a pretty good going town."

"I suppose they have a bank there?" Jessie asked.

"Oh, sure. If I had any money to tuck away, I'd likely be doing business with it. But I don't have spare cash, so when I went looking to borrow some money to tide me over till I could sell off what few of my horses were ready to go to market, they turned me down flat."

"But you did sell your horses?" Ki asked.

"I sold 'em, but it was mostly luck that I come out as good as I did. An old fellow named Miller from down Texas

30

way sends a man out now and again looking for breeding horses, and he just happened to hear about my place. He stopped in and bought eight of my best mares and two good stallions. That's how I got the money I've been running on until now."

"I don't see how you've managed to get enough yearlings to break in." Jessie frowned.

"I don't have all that much trouble, Jessie, at least not yet. There's some pretty fair herds of wild horses on the stretches of flat land and down in the valleys. I buy most of my stock from horse hunters. There's still a few of 'em left, maybe more of them than there is wild horse herds."

"It seems to me you'd need to keep a sort of mixture of horses in different stages of training so that you'd always have some to sell."

"I do that all right," Bruce assured her. "Not that it's easy, not with the wild horse herds worked down like they are on the range. By now the big ranch spreads over east in Colorado and down in Arizona are finding out I've got good stock, but it's going to be a while before I can say I've got a real steady business going."

While they'd been talking, the horses had been moving ahead over the gentle upslope at a steady ground-covering pace. On the rolling rise ahead the grass grew luxuriantly, rippling in the light breeze. To the west the skyline was broken by the humps of a jagged ridge of mountains; to the east the verdant prairie stretched in lazy waves until it met the horizon.

They'd been riding for another half hour or so, talking little, keeping their mounts to the same steady ground-eating pace, when Jessie turned to Bruce and asked, "How much further is it to your place? We haven't stopped to give the horses a good rest for quite a while, and I think it's about time we stopped for a bite to eat."

"Why, we don't have all that much further to go, Miss Jessie," he replied. He pointed ahead, where the ragged line of a rock outcrop broke the level grassland. "Once we get to the top of that ridge up ahead, we'll be able to see my little

31

spread. And it's all downslope the rest of the way."

"Good!" Ki put in. "Because we've been in the saddle long enough for me to get a pretty healthy appetite."

"I think all of us feel the same way," Jessie said. "But I'd just as soon wait to eat until we get to Bruce's ranch. Then we won't have to worry about getting started again."

They rode on, the tiring horses moving a bit more slowly now, even though the upslope was a gentle one. As they neared the crest of the long rise, Bruce turned in his saddle and said to Jessie and Ki, "We're just about there. If you'll look off to the right, you'll be able to see my place."

When they'd gotten close enough to the top of the rise to glimpse the distant terrain beyond, Bruce turned to Jessie and gestured ahead as he said, "Now in just a minute we'll be catching sight of my little place, Miss Jessie. You can—"

He fell silent as he reined his horse to a quick stop. Then he sat motionless in the saddle, his jaw dropping and a puzzled frown forming on his face. He went on, "Why . . . why . . . what in hell's happened? My house is gone! So's my barn! And my horse corrals ain't got a single critter in 'em! I ain't got a thing left in the world!"

Jessie and Ki had quite naturally looked in the direction Bruce had indicated. They were witnesses to the truth of his words. There was nothing in front of them but a barren stretch of prairie grass and the rim of the horizon.

Then Ki took advantage of the athletic skill he'd developed during his education and training in *ninjitsu*, the oriental art of weaponless combat, which requires its practitioners to be able to exercise total physical control. He gripped his saddle horn and drew his folded legs beneath him until he could place his sandal-clad feet on his saddle. Slowly he lifted himself erect, and now he could scan the terrain ahead at a greater height than his companions.

For a moment he gazed at the spot that Bruce had indicated. Then he said soberly, "It saddens me to tell you this, Bruce, but all that I can see are boards and shingles and an overturned stove and some pieces of broken furniture on the ground around the place where you were pointing. I'm afraid that your house and barn have been destroyed."

Bruce stared, speechless, at Ki, his mouth open, his eyes blinking, astonishment mixed with anger reflected on his face. The tone of his voice registered his inability to believe what Ki had said when at last he could bring himself to ask, "You mean that everything on my place has been tore down?"

"That is the way it looks from here," Ki replied.

"Ki, are you sure it's as bad as your description sounded?" Jessie asked.

"I'm afraid it is, Jessie," Ki answered. "But the only way we can be sure is to get closer." He was dropping into his saddle as he spoke, and freeing the reins of his horse. "I couldn't see anything moving, so we should be able to get to the place safely."

Wordlessly, they started their horses moving again. Because Bruce had chosen a little depression in the rolling ground as the site for his home place, they could see nothing until their horses had moved almost halfway up the gently rising slope. Even then, the first objects that came into view were some widely scattered shingles on the ground. A short distance beyond the strewn ground a table lay on its side, its top splintered by an ax into jagged pieces of wood.

Then, as the horses moved higher up the slope ahead, the full scope of destruction became visible. Boards torn from the house and barn lay crisscrossed over the remains of a bed and two or three chairs. Strips of cloth that had once been bedding and clothing littered the ground. Torn-up shreds of paper were scattered everywhere they looked. In one spot a heap of cracked and broken plates and cups and saucers that had been smashed into small bits were strewn willy-nilly. A thin mattress, its ticking sliced into ribbons, had disgorged blobs of its cotton stuffing on the ground around it.

Beyond the house, the barn had suffered a similar vandalism. However, it had been of sturdier construction than the house. Most of its big framing timbers were intact. They lay crisscrossed on the other wreckage, though a few had been split with ax blows, as had some of the barn's wide heavy boards. Only the deeply set posts of the corrals rose above the ground, beyond the remnants of the barn.

No one spoke for several moments. Then Jessie said, "There's going to be a lot of rebuilding needed here, Bruce."

Bruce started to reply, but the knot that had formed in his throat choked his words so badly that neither Jessie nor Ki could understand what he was trying to say. He realized that he was talking gibberish, and fell silent.

"Don't worry," Jessie repeated. "There's too much work waiting to be done to waste time thinking about what's already happened here. It's going to take us quite a while just to clear away this wreckage and see how much of it can be salvaged."

Ki had moved a few paces away from Jessie and Bruce, examining the devastation. Now he asked, "What about your horses, Bruce? Did you leave them in the corrals?"

"Why, sure," Bruce replied. "Charley stayed here—" He stopped short, his face blanching under its tan. "Charley! Oh, my God! What's happened to him?"

Jessie said quickly, "Don't you imagine he's gone to the nearest law officer to get him started after that outlaw gang?"

"Well, that'd make sense, Miss Jessie," Bruce said after a moment of silence. "A-course, we don't have no idea when them bas—" He stopped short and gulped, sat silently for a moment, then went on, "You couldn't call Charley much of a fighter, Miss Jessie. I guess you got to be right; he's gone to get the law out after the renegades that done all this."

"Of course." Jessie nodded. "And I'm sure he'll be back after a while. We don't have any way of knowing when all this damage was done, and from what you've told us it's quite a way to the nearest town."

Ki had been silent for the past few moments, inspecting the wreckage of the house and barn. Now he said, "Hadn't we better begin thinking about getting ready for the night, Jessie? It's late, and as you just said, we don't have any idea when Bruce's helper will be back."

"Of course," Jessie agreed. "But I don't believe we can do much but clear away some of the clutter and make camp. It'll be dark in another hour or so, and there's such a lot to be done that even if we started trying to move this wreckage around we couldn't begin to put a dent in it."

"Then if you and Bruce will tend to the horses," Ki went on, "I'll pick up some wood and get a fire started. Noon was a long time ago, and we'll all feel better after we've eaten and rested."

Bruce had gotten over his first feeling of rage and desolation by this time. He said, "After we've got the horses unsaddled, they'll need to drink, Miss Jessie. I'll tend to that."

"And while you're watering them, I'll give Ki whatever help he needs to get supper started," Jessie told him.

They scattered now, going about the chores of getting settled in for the night. Bruce unsaddled the horses, leaving the headstalls on so that he could lead them easily, and Jessie started toward the spot where Ki was gathering some of the broken shingles for his fire. She'd just reached his side when Bruce's voice rose in a garbled yell. Jessie and Ki turned to look. Bruce was standing beside the wreckage of his cabin, gazing at the ground.

Before Jessie or Ki could reply to his call, Bruce found his voice and shouted, "Charley didn't go looking for a lawman! He's laying here dead. Them outlaws killed him!"

★

Chapter 4

Jessie and Ki wasted no time in hurrying to Bruce's side. He was standing beside the sprawled body of his murdered helper, bending forward, gazing at the dead man. He lay outstretched on his back in a gaping triangle formed by some boards that had fallen on edge in the wreckage of the ruined house and barn.

Neither Jessie nor Ki flinched as they looked down at the man's motionless form, which seemed small and somehow shrunken in death. A black blood-rimmed hole was in his forehead, and on his faded blue shirt two more blots of blood showed where other bullets had plowed into his chest. In one hand his Colt was clutched with his death grip, and his rifle lay close by.

After a moment had ticked away, Bruce said, "There wasn't no call for that outlaw bunch to kill Charley. He never did them any harm, nor I didn't, either."

"I'm sorry, Bruce," Jessie told him. "From what you said when we were talking at the Circle Star, you put a lot of store by your friend."

"He was just a plain good man, Miss Jessie," Bruce replied. He bent down and took the revolver from the dead man's stiffened fingers. Flipping out the Colt's cylinder, he glanced at the bases of the hammer-pocked brass shell cases as he went on, "Every round fired. And I'll bet Charley didn't even draw this pistol till he'd run out of shells for his rifle."

Ki had been standing beside them silently. Now he said, "If you've got a shovel, or if we can find one in all this wreckage, I'll go dig a grave for him, Bruce. The sooner we do it, the better. Just tell me where you want to bury him."

Bruce was silent for a moment; then he turned and pointed to a rock outcrop that surfaced at the end of a wide grassed strip a short distance from the wrecked buildings.

"I guess over yonder, just before you get to them rocks," he said. "There's soft dirt all this side of 'em. I'll fetch you a shovel. I had two good ones in the barn that bunch of outlaws wrecked, so I oughta be able to find one of 'em. But you don't have to do the digging, Ki. Charley wasn't just somebody who worked for me. Oh, sure, he was my hired hand, but he was my friend, too. I figure I owe it to him to put down his grave."

"No, Bruce," Jessie said, her voice both sympathetic and stern. "Let Ki do the digging. We'll have to get your helper ready to be buried. I'll give you a hand wrapping him in a quilt or blanket or whatever you might want to cover him with before you put him in the grave."

"I don't rightly know what's left to use, Miss Jessie." Bruce frowned. "But even if things are all upside-down and scattered around, I reckon I can go through this mess and find a blanket or some oilcloth or something like that."

"We'll get busy, then," Jessie went on. "I'll help you look for something to cover him with. There'll be time after we've finished burying him for us to fix some sort of shakedown where we can sleep tonight. We're all hungry and tired, so before we turn in we'd better eat a bite. While we're eating, we can decide what our next move will be."

Their unhappy task of burying Bruce's helper was soon finished. Walking in silence away from the small rectangle of freshly turned earth that now stood out against the green prairie grass, they returned to the wreckage of the house and barn. They reached the edge of the untidy sprawl of broken, splintered boards that had been buildings and the bits and pieces that remained of the sparse furnishings of the house. Bruce tossed the spade he'd been carrying onto the heap and turned to face Jessie and Ki.

"After that job we've just done, I don't have much of an appetite," he said. "You and Ki go ahead and eat, Jessie. Turn in whenever you feel like it. I think I better take a little walk and try to get over being so cussed mad before I bust."

Jessie spoke quickly; her voice was sympathetic but firm. "Wait a minute, Bruce. I can't say that I blame you for feeling the way you do, but you've worked hard to start your horse ranch, and from what you told me when you came to the Circle Star, you're starting to make this place pay. Are you going to let one setback make you give up?"

"You might call it a setback," Bruce replied. "But I call it being ruined. After all the work I've put in, and poor old Charley being killed—"

Jessie did not allow him to finish. "Nothing that happened here was your fault, so don't begin blaming yourself. Your friend's dead, and that means he's gone forever. I know how you feel, because I felt the same way when my father was murdered. But there's nothing you can do to change what's already happened."

"Oh, I know you're right, Miss Jessie." He nodded. "But suppose this was to happen at the Circle Star?"

Jessie disliked what she knew she must say, but made herself say it anyway as she replied, "It has happened there, Bruce, in case you've forgotten. And even if you don't feel hungry, all three of us have to eat if we expect to stay strong enough to get any work done."

"I'm sorry, Miss Jessie," Bruce said. "But all this—"

"All this won't change unless we work at it," Jessie went on. She turned to Ki and said, "Ki, will you get our saddle rations? I'm sure there's enough left for us to make some sort of a pickup meal."

39

"You and Ki go ahead and eat," Bruce told Jessie as Ki turned away and started toward the horses. "Right now there's a lump in my gullet so big that I don't feel like I could choke down a single bite."

"I can understand that, of course," Jessie said. "And even if it won't keep you from feeling sad about losing your helper, I'll say right now that what you've told me and what I've seen on this trip convinces me that you haven't changed from the way you were on the Circle Star."

"You're saying—" he began.

Jessie broke in before Bruce could finish his question. "I'm saying that I'll see to you getting the money you need to fix up your spread and get it working again."

"Well, I guess that's the best news I could have, and I sure needed it. Even feeling bad as I do about Charley, maybe I'll sleep a lot better tonight because you said what you did."

"I know you're not yourself right now, Bruce," Jessie went on. "And I hope you'll eat something, even if you have to force yourself to do it. There's a lot of work waiting for us. If you want to get your horse herd back from those outlaws, you've got to keep up your strength."

"There's six of the outlaws, and three of us." Bruce frowned. "That's two-to-one odds. And we still don't know for sure where they headed."

"Ki and I have faced worse odds," Jessie said. "And you might not remember, but Ki's one of the best trackers you'll find anywhere."

"If we're going to go after them, hadn't we better set out right now, Miss Jessie?" Bruce asked. "Those killers have got too good of a start on us, and they're likely to put a lot of miles between us and them by daylight."

"We don't have much choice," Jessie pointed out. "There's only about an hour of daylight left, and we certainly can't follow their trail in the dark. Besides, Ki and I need you to give us some idea of the way the land lays. And the best time to do that is right now."

40

"Why, hereabouts it's fine. Everyplace else, it's just about the same raw kind of country we rode across coming up here from your ranch, Miss Jessie," he replied. "Between the ridges and the humps and a stand of big high mesas there's some pretty fair little pieces of rangeland like right here, where a man can run cattle or horses without being afraid the graze will go dry or the water dry up."

"From the little of it I've seen, your place just suits what you're doing," Jessie said. "It's not big enough to farm or run cattle on, but for training horses, it's just right."

"About the worst you can say is that it ain't a place where there's a lot of water." Bruce frowned. "I got a good spring, enough flow for a pretty good-sized bunch of horses, but like you said, it ain't easy to find good crop or cattle country."

While Bruce was speaking, Ki had returned carrying a bulging flour sack. When Bruce fell silent, he added quickly, "What you're really saying is that the place we'll be looking for is apt to be pretty much like yours."

"Oh, sure. I never have seen it, but I figure it's got to be on top of one of the mesas or down in a wide valley like here. Except it ain't likely to be as big, so I sorta figure it's a mesa top."

"How many men do you think there'd be in the gang?" Ki asked.

"You'd know as much about that as I do, Ki. There's times when I've seen five, maybe six, riding past, but when push comes to shove, I can't even prove for sure that they're outlaws. Me and Charley kept trying to figure out whether we ought to tip off the law to them, but we didn't have a thing to go on. It wasn't till just a little while back we figured out where their hideout just about had to be."

"I'm sure that you had enough on your hands without doing what the Nevada authorities should've been looking after." Jessie frowned. "I know you well enough to realize you're not the kind who sees ghosts under the bed at night."

"Well, Miss Jessie, in all the places I've been since I pushed out on my own, I've run across a badman or two.

41

And most of the time you can tell them from a regular cowhand. But you and Ki must've found that out for yourselves after all the crooks you've gone after since your daddy got killed."

Jessie had stepped over to Ki's side; they were both digging into the ration sack. Jessie found the bundle of sliced summer sausage and the bag of big soda crackers that served as the base of their saddle rations. She was busy putting slices of sausage between crackers and did not reply at once. After she'd made sandwiches for Ki and Bruce and one for herself, she picked up their conversation.

"What you were just saying is true, Bruce." She nodded. "And I'll agree that a lot of outlaws give themselves away. But surely you must have some good reason for believing that the men we were talking about are really outlaws."

"Outside of the way they acted, never coming close to my place here and swapping hellos, most of what I'm going by is saloon talk." Bruce frowned. "But you know yourself that the kind of hunch I got is right more times than it is wrong where outlaws're concerned."

"Judging by what you've told us about the way they behaved, I'm sure you're right," Jessie agreed. "And it's a shame there are no lawmen to help around here."

"Lawmen's scarcer than hen's teeth in Nevada Territory," Bruce said. "One reason for that is, there's a bunch of only about twenty that works for the Territory. They call theirselves the Territorial Rangers, but they mostly keep busy up north, between here and Tonopah, where there's all them new gold mines. What it comes down to is that hereabouts a man's just about got to be his own law."

Jessie nodded. "It's certainly nothing new in raw country like this."

"A good part of what I've heard about that bunch is just saloon talk," Bruce went on. "Bits and pieces I've picked up when I was having a drink at one of the places in Navajo Spring or Cedar City."

"You've said you found out where their hideout is," Ki remarked. "But do you know whether it has a house, or any kind of shelter on it?"

"Now, that I can't tell you, Ki," Bruce replied. "With all the work that me and Charley has had to get done here, we didn't have time to tend to much besides our own business. Now and then a horse I'm training strays off, so I do considerable riding around looking for it, and if that bunch has got a house, I never have run across it."

"You'd know the general lay of the land, though, with all the riding after strays you said you've done," Jessie said. "You'd surely have noticed a house, but you might've missed seeing a box canyon or the opening of a cave."

"I was just about to say there was caves and canyons galore in that rough country eastwards along the big river, Miss Jessie," Bruce said. "But most of the decent country's inside the big Paiute reservation."

"I didn't even know there was an Indian reservation anywhere around here." Jessie frowned.

At almost the same moment Ki asked, "How much of a ride is it to that reservation?"

Bruce answered Ki's question first. He said, "A day if you push a mite, a day and a half if you want to go easy on your horse. I'd bet a silver dollar to a plug of tobacco that the best place where we can start looking for the horse thieves is a big double mesa that's just past that Paiute reservation."

"A double mesa?" Jessie frowned.

"Well, that's what I call it," Bruce replied. "It's a little mesa that's joined up with a bigger one. Or maybe I better say a higher one. If you'd look at from up above someplace, or maybe in a balloon, it'd be like an eight."

"Well, that makes sense." Jessie smiled. "But you said you've never had any trouble with the Indians."

"Not so's you'd notice," Bruce told her. "But there ain't enough Paiutes left to bother a man. Now, the Chiricahuas that's just about run 'em off their own reservation are right mean, but they don't bother me, either."

"What you're saying is that you don't bother them and they don't bother you," Ki broke in.

"That's about the size of it," he agreed.

"Let's get back to the outlaws," Jessie said. "This trail you've mentioned that you think will get us to their hideout isn't the one we followed coming up here, then?"

Bruce shook his head as he replied, "What occurs to me is the land on top of a mesa's pretty generally good, except maybe if it hasn't got water. I'd imagine it's pretty level, mostly there's level land up above the river canyon where the Paiute reservation is and before you'd hit the gold country up further north. Money changes hands pretty free around where there's gold mines, and I sorta figured that mesa's a place a bunch of outlaws might head, especially when money's free like it is all around there."

"Yes, I know about the big boom that started around Tonopah." Jessie nodded. "But from what little information I've been able to get I'd say it's not a stampede, but sort of an off-and-on boom."

"I'm sure you know what Jessie means," Ki put in. "Some lucky miner hits a rich lode and the news spreads and other miners rush to it. And the farmers and ranchers hurry to bring their stock where they know they'll get a good price for it. Then the ore in the discovery lode peters out and the boom starts somewhere else where another miner's found a new lode."

"That's about the way it's been, all right," Bruce agreed. "But I've sold a lot of horses wherever there's even been a whisper of a new gold find. Even if I'd've had a bigger herd I could've sold 'em in a minute. The trouble is, the price I got to pay for good horseflesh keeps going up and up. That's why I went to the Circle Star to ask you for a loan. Once I get away from living hand-to-mouth, this little spread oughta do real well."

"What you're really saying is that you need operating capital, Bruce," Jessie told him. "But now you're going to need more money than you'd thought, because you'll have to rebuild your house and barn. And how long is it going to take you to train the first horses you'll need to sell?"

"Why I can generally break and train a wild horse in two or three months," he replied. "But if I'm working a little bunch of 'em all at once it takes maybe two or three times as long."

"Then you'll need two or three times as much money to get started," Jessie said.

"I guess that's how you'd have to put it." Bruce nodded. "But I sure hope you figure I know enough to come out of this right-side-up, Miss Jessie."

"Of course you do," Jessie told him. "But before you start your horse ranch, something's going to have to be done about those outlaws who raided you and put you out of business. If they're not stopped now, they'll very likely wait until you've trained a new bunch of horses and raid your place again."

"That's something I don't want to see happen," Bruce said. "And what I aim to do when I get another spread put together is to buy me one of those newfangled Gatling guns that'll scatter more lead around than a dozen men can."

"And it might not be such a bad thing to have," Ki agreed. "All you'd have to do would be to see that the word spread about you being ready to use it on horse thieves."

"Well, it's something to think about," Jessie said. "But we don't have a Gatling gun now, and we've got to move quickly if we expect to catch up with those horse thieves. Ki, you're better at tracking than Bruce and me combined. Do you think you can find their trail and keep us on it?"

"I can try my best," he replied. "If you and Bruce will take care of getting our gear in your saddlebags, I'll do some circling around in the direction they've taken. You and Bruce keep an eye on me. I'll wave when I'm sure I've picked up their tracks."

Jessie nodded, and Ki started for the tethered horses. He was in the saddle and beginning to ride around what remained of Bruce's house and barn before Jessie and Bruce reached their own horses. By the time they'd finished stowing the diminished bundles of leftover food in their saddlebags, his zigzag path had taken Ki a good distance across the flatland. Jessie and Bruce mounted up to follow him. They did not feel any need to hurry, but started their horses into a steady walk in the direction Ki had chosen.

They'd almost caught up with him when Ki yanked his reins sharply to one side and bent low in his saddle to study the ground in front of him. He began reining his horse in a zigzag pattern, from one side to the other, continuing to keep his eyes on the ground. Just before Jessie and Bruce reached him, Ki brought his mount to a halt and settled back in his saddle. He waited until Jessie and Bruce were only a few yards distant before he spoke.

"I can't be completely positive yet, but I'm reasonably sure that I can see what's happened," Ki said. "The gang that killed your helper must've split up after they rode away from your house, Bruce."

"You mean there's more than one trail now?" Bruce asked.

Ki nodded as he went on, "It's a pretty common move outlaws make when they've pulled off a job, or killed somebody like they did your friend. They did a lot of milling around right here. The outlaws' tracks and those your horses left are so mixed up that it's hard to tell just what they did."

"But you're as sure as it's possible to be?" Bruce tried to make his question sound casual, but his efforts did not hide the undertone of eager anxiety in his voice.

"Well, on that last spot of clear ground we crossed further back I found two different hoofprints that I can't be mixed up about," Ki replied. "And I'm pretty sure my guess they split up here is right."

Jessie had realized at once what Ki was trying to explain to Bruce. Even before he pointed to the prints of horses' iron-shod hooves pocking the arid soil, she'd seen the crescent-shaped marks cutting into its baked surface.

Ki went on, "The shoe on one of the horses that left these prints has lost the front calk off its forefoot. And the shoes on one of the other horses are brand new. Then when I picked up the trail up ahead, the prints of the horse that has the new shoes just weren't with the others. I'm not certain how many other riders there were, because the other hoofprints don't have any marks that I could pick out for sure."

"That's good enough to satisfy me, Ki," Jessie said. "It must mean just what you figured out, that the horse with the new shoes isn't with the others. And if it's not, the chances are good that the outlaws have split up. That means we're going to have to split up, too."

Bruce shook his head as he said, "I don't like that idea at all. Isn't there anything else we can do? I can't let you and Ki do what you're figuring on. Just coming here with me all the way from the Circle Star's more'n any help I've got a right to expect. If there's gunfighting—"

"If there's gunfighting, neither Ki nor I will be facing something we haven't run into before," Jessie said. "Bruce, one of the first lessons I learned from my father was that it's a mistake to do anything only halfway. I've told you that Ki and I will help you get your horse ranch back in good shape, and that's just what we intend to do."

"But, Miss Jessie—" he began.

"No buts, ifs, or maybes," she broke in. "And we won't mention it again." Before Bruce could carry his protest further, she turned to Ki and went on, "If you're even reasonably sure we've found the trail we're looking for, let's start following it."

★

Chapter 5

"Which one of these forks do you think we should take, Bruce?" Jessie asked as she and Ki reined in beside him.

Bruce shook his head as he replied, "There's no horse tracks I can make out on either one of 'em. A while back the horse thieves never did come this way. It's as new a trail to me as it is to you, I reckon."

"I'm sure either one of them will get us to the top of the mesa." Jessie frowned as she scanned the terrain. "So let's just pick out one and ride on up. Once we get on level ground again, we ought to pick up the trail we need to follow."

She spoke without taking her eyes off the two hoof-pocked strips of beaten earth that formed a rough Y on the ground where they'd pulled up their horses. The forks separated widely, one going to their right, the other to the left. Both bore faint hoofprints, but none of the prints offered a clue as to when they had been made, for all of them were robbed of detail by the coarseness of the bare soil.

For the past half hour Jessie had been riding in the lead. She'd stopped at the point where the trail branched and was now looking from one of the narrow strips of beaten earth to the other. Neither of the two offered any clue as to which was the one chosen by the outlaws, or even by the greater number of travelers who'd used it.

Ki's eyes moved just as Jessie's did. Both of them were examining and comparing the trail forks where they'd stopped. After Ki had finished his examination, he shook his head and turned to Jessie.

"We're agreed on one thing, Jessie," he said. "I can't see any difference between the two, either. And something else has just occurred to me. For the last mile or so we haven't seen a print of that horse with the missing calk on one shoe."

"I guess we're all thinking the same thing, then," Bruce said slowly. "The outlaws must've have turned off the trail somewhere behind us, and we missed seeing the place where they left it."

Jessie went on, "It's a shame that the horse droppings aren't any help. In this desert country they dry too fast. It's just not possible to tell which are fresh and which have been on the ground for weeks, maybe months."

"Before either one of you asks, I'll tell you right flat-out that I'm as stumped as you are," Bruce admitted. "I never was all that good at reading sign, unless it's marked real plain. There's been too many times to count when I've tried to follow after a horse that's strayed up here, and I couldn't for the life of me tell which prints was old and which ones had been left by the critter I was looking for."

"We'd better backtrack, then," Jessie suggested. "Even after we pick up the outlaws' tracks again, we won't be able to cover very much ground before it's too dark to see anything."

"Remember, Jessie, outlaws have a habit of getting off a trail now and then," Ki said thoughtfully. "They'll ride alongside it for a while, maybe cross it a time or two, just to confuse anybody who might be following them."

"You know I don't forget things like that, Ki," she told him. "But I do think that before it gets too dark to see tracks easily, we'd better make sure this trail we're on is the one we're looking for."

"I'd say it's six of one and a half-dozen of the other," Bruce suggested. "But we've got an hour, maybe as much as two hours of daylight left, and it'd sure be a pity to have it go to waste."

Jessie nodded. "Of course. We've got to be sure we're following the right tracks. Once we're satisfied that we're on the right trail, we can stop for the night and start tracking again at daylight." Turning to Ki, she went on, "A minute or so ago, you said that you'd just gone a little distance along the right-hand fork of the river. Since you've already covered part of it, it'll save time if you go to where you turned back and follow the stream a little further. We need to make sure they didn't ride in the water for a while, to hide their tracks. Bruce and I can split up and scout both these forks to see if they took one of them."

"I'm not sure I like the idea of separating, Jessie." Ki frowned. "It'll be dark in just a couple of hours."

"That's all the more reason why we can't lose too much time, Ki," Jessie reminded him. "And if we're heading in the wrong direction, we'd better know it now than later."

Ki nodded and said, "Of course. There's still enough daylight left for me to do that, and I won't turn back to join you till it's dark."

"How'll we meet in the dark after we're separated?" Bruce frowned. "Jessie and I might hit a hot trail. I don't think you're as likely to as we are, and if we should happen to get on a good lead, we'll—"

"Don't worry," Jessie broke in. "Ki and I have used shot signals before." Turning back to Ki, she went on, "If you don't get back before it's pitch dark, I'll wait a while and fire one shot. That'll set your direction for you."

"Suppose the outlaws are still somewhere close by?" Bruce asked. "If they hear shooting, they'll—"

"Turn back to follow us?" Jessie broke in. "It might help us if they do, Bruce. It'd certainly save us the time we're having to spend trying to find their trail. And any shots Ki hears will bring him back to us in a hurry."

"Everything's settled, then," Ki said. He glanced at their shadows on the prairie, then flicked his eyes at the sun, which was barely a hand-span above the horizon line. He went on, "We've still got about an hour of daylight left. If we have any luck, that much time will give us a lot of leeway."

Jessie nodded, then she said, "We'll both be covering about the same distance before it gets too dark to move. But just to avoid confusion, let's not use shot signals, Ki, and if you run into the trail left by those horse thieves, come back to this place where we are now. If we find the trail, we'll do the same thing. We'll camp here tonight and pick up whatever trail we find in the morning."

"Of course," Ki agreed. "Now, if we're going to make the best use of what daylight's left, we'd better be moving."

While Ki spoke, he was reining his mount around. He toed the horse ahead. Before he started down the long slope leading to the river, he glanced back at Jessie and Bruce and saw that they were starting. Then he kept his mount moving briskly for the short time required to reach the point where he'd turned back earlier.

As Ki returned to the river, he rode at a wider angle than he'd taken when coming to rejoin Jessie and Bruce. He concentrated on studying his surroundings as he moved across the steep downslope, but saw no signs that the outlaws had passed over any of it. He reached the ancient valley cut by the river as it had flooded and drained away the soil during the uncounted years of its history.

Keeping his horse to a slow walk, he moved at a long slant toward the sinuous river, his eyes searching the mostly barren ground. He reached the sharper downslope leading to the stream and leaned back in his saddle while his horse braced its hind legs and started sliding down. Just short of the water's edge, Ki reined in to study the trail that ran beside the riverbank.

At the point where he had stopped, the surface of the stream was smooth and the water itself was dark. Ki shook his head when he saw the smoothly unbroken surface, a sure indication of a stretch of deep water and a strong current. He had no desire to wade his mount into it.

Reining in, Ki stood up in his stirrups and looked ahead. A hundred yards or so in front of him Ki saw the bubbling froth on the water's surface that marked the end of the deep hole. He touched the horse's flank with his toes and kept his eyes on the river while the animal stepped slowly along the bank. As he'd been certain they would, the murky depths began to grow lighter, and soon he could see the scoured tops of big boulders. Another fifty or sixty yards farther the big hole came to an end in swirls of froth, and beyond the froth the brighter hue of shallow water was visible.

When Ki could see the rocky bottom clearly he twitched the reins to stop his horse and dropped from the saddle. Leading the horse to the water's edge, he stood gazing at the stream. A few paces from the water's edge he noticed a shining glint on the river bottom. He was sure that the glitter could only be silver.

Stepping into the knee-deep water, Ki waded toward the shimmering object and bent to pick it up. As his fingers touched the surface, he realized that the water was deeper than he'd thought it to be, and that plunging his arm into the stream would wet his *shuriken* in their leather case strapped to his forearm. Unbuckling the strap, he removed the case and dropped it into the capacious pocket of his jacket.

He bent again to pick up the gleaming bit of silver and found when he'd pulled it from the river that it was the badly tarnished insignia, a pair of silver bars, that in the army identified the rank of captain. He looked at it for a moment, then tucked it into a saddlebag.

In his saddle again and across the stream, Ki turned the horse along the stream's bank. He watched the terrain even more closely now, trying to locate the place where he'd turned back to rejoin Jessie and Bruce. When he saw the spot he'd marked in his memory, he altered his direction to retrace his former path.

Ki looked back only once, to note the landmarks that would be his guide to the point where he'd entered the water. His glance told him that his time to search was limited, for the sun was dropping low toward the horizon and the sky was already reflecting the reddening blush that came before sunset.

In his absorption with the need to move quickly, Ki did not follow his usual habit of scanning his surroundings when riding over unfamiliar terrain. The shot that echoed as a bullet raised a small fountain of water only inches away from his horse's forelegs took him by surprise. Leaning forward, he reached for his rifle in its saddle scabbard. He had his hand on the throat of the rifle stock when a man's guttural voice sounded from a small stand of bushes on the bank just ahead of him.

"Leave gun! Hold out hands! Not move!"

Ki recognized instantly the authority in the tone of the invisible man who'd spoken. He had faced such situations many times before, during the years when he and Jessie were battling the sinister European cartel that had been responsible for Alex Starbuck's murder. He obeyed the command, freezing in his saddle, his body still leaning forward, as he lifted his hands slowly until his arms were extended at his sides.

Splashes sounded in the river behind him. Ki did not turn to look, for his attention was now concentrated on finding the man ahead, who'd issued the commands. The splashes in back of him tapered off and ended. A brawny brown-skinned arm brushed past Ki's thigh and yanked his rifle from its saddle scabbard.

At almost the same instant a bronze-skinned Indian stepped from the place where he'd been hidden, behind a jagged-edged boulder that rose two or three paces away from the riverbank. The rifle he held leveled across his chest was aimed directly and steadily at Ki.

Ki frowned as his eyes flicked over the Indian on the riverbank. Though he was familiar with the tribal characteristics of a dozen of the score or more of Indian tribes active in the West, Ki did not recognize the man's tribal origin. He did not have the hawklike nose and protruding chin that characterized the tribes of the northern plains, nor were his nose and chin rounded like the Indians of the arid Southwest. Ki could get no hint from his captor's clothing, for he wore only a breechclout.

"Off horse," the Indian commanded.

Berating himself silently for the inattention that had put him in his unpleasant situation, Ki obeyed. Still keeping his eyes on the Indian standing on the bank, he levered out of the saddle and lowered himself into the knee-deep stream. Even when he heard splashes behind him, Ki did not move; nor did he try to look around when he felt the muzzle of a rifle dig into his back. Then the man on the riverbank barked a guttural order in a tongue that Ki did not understand, although he was familiar with a half-dozen Indian languages.

"Walk slow to bank," the man behind him ordered, prodding Ki none too gently with the muzzle of his rifle.

Ki had no choice but to obey. He began pushing through the knee-deep stream. As he advanced, his eyes opened wider, for still more Indians were emerging from the scant brush cover where they had somehow managed to hide unseen.

Before Ki reached the shore, there were eight of them, standing in a rough semicircle behind the man who was obviously their leader. Only two or three of them carried rifles. The others were armed with head-high spears; none of them wore war paint. Ki stepped up on the low bank and faced their leader. Behind him water splashed as the Indian following him left the river. Once again Ki felt the muzzle of the man's rifle dig into his back.

"You look of our people, but you are not," the Indian facing Ki said.

When Ki did not reply at once, the man who had spoken turned to one of the men behind him and for a moment the two Indians talked in their native language. Their conversation was broken several times by gestures as the man being questioned turned to wave toward the river, or pointed at Ki and nodded his head, or replied to the leader.

At last the leader turned back to Ki and said, "You were here before. It will do you no good to lie to me. The man I was talking with saw you. He came to our village to tell me that there were strangers coming on our reservation."

"I have no reason to lie," Ki replied. "Yes, I am with others. We are trying to catch horse thieves who have stolen many horses from one of them."

"Where are these people now?" the Indian asked.

"Several miles from here," Ki answered. "On the high mesa, waiting for me to return to join them."

"Are they like you?" The Indian frowned. "You and your people must be from far away. I have seen none like you before now."

"I am the only one of them who is not of this country," Ki replied. "My own people are far across the sea. We are called Japanese."

"Then why you are here?"

Risking a gesture, Ki waved toward the escarpments rising in the west as he replied, "I have already told you why. I have come here to help the people I am traveling with to find horses that have been stolen from one of them."

"Do you say that we steal horses?" the Indian asked, his voice grating angrily.

Ki shook his head. "I meant nothing of that kind. We know it was not your people who stole the horses. It was outlaws of our own people."

"If you do not blame us, why do you come here? This land, this river, is reservation for only our people."

"We didn't have any way to know that," Ki replied. "We were trying to find the horses and the men who stole them

56

by their tracks. We lost the hoofprints several miles downstream along the river. Now that I know a bunch of horse thieves wouldn't've come here, I'll be glad to turn around and get off your land just as fast—"

Ki broke off as an angry yell sounded from behind him. The leader raised his head and started toward the water's edge. Ki risked turning around to look at the man who'd been holding his horse.

Now the Indian was standing beside Ki's horse. He held the saddlebags in one hand and was shouting excitedly in his own language as he waved the silver bars that Ki had dropped into the bag after he'd picked up the army insignia from the river.

Before Ki could turn back to the leader, the Indian with the rifle had reached his side and was jamming the muzzle into Ki's chest. His eyes were on the silver bars. He said something in his own tongue to the man who'd found the army insignia. The second man replied in the Indians' tongue, bobbing his head as he spoke, then he turned back to Ki.

"You lie about horses you look for!" the man with the gun snapped as he jabbed the muzzle of his rifle into Ki's chest. "You are soldier, you come to spy!"

"That's not true!" Ki protested. "I found those silver bars in the river while I was riding here, where some army officer had lost them! I'm not a soldier, I've already told you that I'm not even from this country!"

"More lies!" the Indian said angrily. "Our warriors have fought soldiers many times! We know the white war chiefs wear two bars of silver! You come here now to learn how many warriors our people have, and find where we have built our village. Then you will go back and tell what you have found to your soldiers. They will bring the big thunder guns here to make war on us! To kill all of us so you can have our land!"

"Look at me!" Ki said. "Do I look like a white man? I am not of this country, I have no quarrel with your people!"

"Lies! Lies! Lies! Nothing you say is true!" The Indian's voice was less strident now, but its angry tone remained much the same as he went on, "We will make you talk! We have not forgotten the old ways of fire and hot stones on a man's belly to make him tell us what we want to know!"

Before Ki could speak again, the Indian was gesturing to his companions. They swarmed over Ki, and though he managed to send the first few sprawling with his adroit *hiji* and *kote* blows and his *mashai-geri* and *seashi* kicks, there were too many for even a *karateka* of his skill to handle. Their muscles were almost as strong and supple as Ki's, and the struggle lasted only a few minutes before they had brought him down.

At the leader's command, they pulled his arms and legs out straight. Some of the Indian warriors surrounding him stepped onto each of Ki's limbs, effectively pinning him to the ground. Ki stopped struggling then, and lay motionless, wondering what would now be in store for him.

Turning to his men, the Indian leader began talking to them. Occasionally one of the warriors would break into the man's flow of speech with what was obviously a question, and a few words would be exchanged between them. Ki could not understand their language, and could make nothing from the gestures that accompanied the lengthy harangue. At last the Indian leader turned and looked down at him.

"We will take you with us to our village," he told Ki. "And we will keep you there while I send men to scout the land around. If they find no soldiers waiting to attack us, and if they see that these people you have told us you are traveling with are as you say, we will set you free. If you have lied to us, you will die."

"Wait a minute!" Ki protested. "If you really intend to turn me loose, why can't you let me go with one of these scouting parties you say you'll send out? I have told you nothing but the truth! I found those army shoulder-bars laying on the bottom of the river, a little way back along the trail on my way here. I am not a soldier! You only have to look at me to see that!"

"I have not said you are a soldier," the man replied. "I have said you are a scout, and we know your army well from our fights with it. Their scouts are not always soldiers. You do not need to be afraid. I will do as I told you. Now, I will listen to you no more until my own people have proved you are what you say you are."

Then the leader bound Ki's arms and legs with supple leather thongs and two of the warriors threw him roughly across the back of his horse. With Ki's head hanging on one side of the horse, his legs dangling on the other, and one of the Indians leading the animal, the group started moving upriver on the narrow path beside its bank.

★

Chapter 6

For the first few minutes after the men who'd captured him
started on the trail, Ki had not only been angry, he'd been
more than a little uncomfortable. Though he'd landed across
his saddle, there was a great difference between straddling it
in normal fashion and hanging across it like a saddle blanket.
His legs swayed in one direction while his head bobbed in
another, and the ridge of his saddle horn rising on one side
pressed his stomach muscles like a dull knife.

Gradually Ki's anger faded as his supple muscles adjusted
to the new and unaccustomed strains they were feeling and
he called his *karateka* training into use. He discovered that
if he focused his gaze intently for a few moments at a
time on the bare, featureless earth of the rock-studded trail,
he could overcome the dizzying effects of being bound,
bent helplessly horizontal, and in almost constant movement as his head swayed on one side and his feet on the
other.

Once adjusted to his unpleasant circumstances, Ki discovered that by bending his neck backward to the utmost
and turning his head from one side to the other he could
find landmarks along the high walls of the canyon during the moments when he took his gaze off his immediate

61

surroundings. Now he began looking for them and storing them in his memory: oversized boulders, zigzag cracks, and small crevasses, which occasionally supported sparse stands of thin-stalked weeds, now and then a small twisted-trunk sapling.

Even while his mind was registering what few details were offered by the barren land, Ki was planning the strategies that he could use when the opportunity arrived to escape from his captors. He had no doubt that such a time would come.

After covering what he estimated to be a bit less than a half mile, Ki began catching sight of crude, sparsely thatched huts. They stood higgledy-piggledy on both sides of the trail. Most of them huddled close to the high walls of the canyon, but a handful of the huts had been built on the strip of land between the trail and the riverbank. Small fires burned in front of several of the little hovels, bright in the shadowed canyon. Now and again Ki caught a glimpse of the Paiutes who lived in them.

Unlike the breechclout-clad warriors who had captured him, the few Indian men around the huts wore baggy coats of loosely woven cotton that hung almost to their knees. The women outnumbered the men, and were clad in the same type of loose garments, but theirs were longer, covering their legs to mid-calf. Neither the men nor the women gave any signs that they noticed the Indians who formed the little group clustered around Ki. It was as though they were invisible or that they did not really exist.

As the little procession moved farther along the trail, the huts were fewer and more widely spaced. Ki had no landmarks by which to judge distance, but his guess was that the men who'd made him their prisoner had covered a bit more than two miles since his first unlucky encounter with them at the river.

A short time after he'd made his estimate of the distance he'd been carried, the trail swerved away from the river and angled through a wide gap in the bluff beside the stream, onto level ground that stretched from wall to wall of high sandstone cliffs, which formed a roughly oval box canyon. Here, out of the narrow shadowed crevasse in which the river ran, the light was still good, though the sun was hanging low now, only a short distance above the big depression's high walls.

By twisting his neck around, Ki could glimpse several buffalo-hide tepees on a low rise at the far end of the canyon. Then the leader veered to change their course, and as the men carrying Ki followed them, more dwellings came into Ki's field of vision. They were not tepees, but make-shift hovels of the same kind he'd seen along the trail, huts spaced well apart from one another across the canyon floor. Tetherless horses grazed on the scant vegetation beyond them. As the group reached the center of the canyon, Ki could occasionally catch sight of men hurrying toward the band that had captured him.

Then the Indians' leader stopped and gestured in silent command. The man who'd been leading the horse lifted Ki's shoulders and dragged him from the saddle, letting him fall to the ground with a thud.

When he landed on the hard-baked soil, Ki closed his eyes and lay motionless, making no effort to get to his feet. From the distant shouts that reached his ears and the louder replies made by the Indians surrounding him, he knew that he had become the center of attraction. As the distant shouts became fewer and fewer and the voices around him grew louder, he could tell from their angry tones that he was surrounded by enemies.

After a few moments the shouts died away and Ki could hear a confused babble of guttural voices. They spoke con-versationally, in a language strange to Ki, and there were so many men talking that Ki could not separate them by their voices any more than he could understand what they were saying. Ki still did not move; nor did he open his eyes at once. Then, as the guttural chatter around him increased rather than diminished, he risked cracking his eyelids to the narrowest possible slits. Now that he could see as well as hear, Ki realized that his deductions had been surprisingly accurate.

He was indeed surrounded by the redskins, who appeared to be engaged in some sort of an argument. Aware that sooner or later he would be forced to open his eyes fully, Ki did so now. With his field of vision increased, he could see that there were a dozen or more Indian warriors standing bunched around him. They were paying no attention to him. In groups of three or four they were standing face-to-face, their voices were raised, some of them were waving their arms and gesturing, each trying to shout down the other. To Ki, it appeared that the discussion was on the verge of breaking into an all-out fight.

Before the tensions grew taut enough to snap, a loud shout overrode the din. The Indians visible to Ki turned, then parted as one of their number began pushing through the ragged circle and stopped beside Ki's recumbent form. Ki got only a glimpse of the man who'd broken through the clusters of Indians, but that fleeting look told him that the newcomer's ornate necklace of animal teeth, bleached bird bones, and small dabs of rarely seen trade turquoise and coral must mark him as a tribal chief.

Ki closed his eyes quickly. He heard the soft susurrus of moccasined feet on the baked ground come close to him and stop. The voice of the chief sounded above Ki's head. The words he heard meant nothing to Ki, but the tone of the Indian's voice told him that orders were being given.

Then Ki heard the whispery sounds of the party's moccasined feet moving away. When the fading voices of the Indians dropped into silence, he cracked his lids open a slit and watched the little group until it veered away from the limited area which he could scan. He'd barely lost sight of the group of moving Indians when from the opposite direction, outside of his range of vision but near enough to startle him, the sudden unexpected noise of scraping feet warned him to close his eyes quickly.

Ki felt rough hands close on his bound ankles, then other hands slid under his shoulders and groped for his armpits. Guided by his instincts, Ki instantly relaxed all his muscles. He let his body sag when he was raised from the ground, and as the men who'd lifted him moved to carry him, he swayed a bit from side to side as an unconscious person would be expected to do.

Mustering every scrap of control he possessed, Ki kept his eyes closed to slits and let his muscles remain limp while the men carried him. They moved steadily, but in his uncomfortable position Ki had no real way to judge distance. When at last they stopped, his captors did not drop him to the ground. The man who'd been carrying his feet released his hold, and as Ki balanced on his own feet, the man who'd been gripping his ankles moved away. Though his footsteps grated lightly on the hard soil, Ki's keen ears told him that the Indian took only a few steps.

Now the men who still supported Ki lifted him by the armpits and dragged him for a few paces across the hard, dry ground. Ki maintained his feigned unconsciousness, letting his head droop, his eyes still closed. Ki felt the hands of one of the Indians grab his midsection and half-turn him as his companion twisted Ki's shoulders.

Unexpectedly, Ki felt himself being lifted by the armpits and pushed backward. Suddenly his back encountered something solid. Then as the Indians shoved him against the object he'd felt and lifted his feet while pushing him, Ki realized that he was being pinned against a high stake set deeply into the iron-hard soil. He felt the bite of rope around his chest as the Indian binding him pulled it tight, its scraping against the post sounding loud in his ears.

Ki sagged forward, trying to put a little space between his spine and the post, but his captors pulled the bond tight and he heard the soft whispering scrape of knots being tied. The men lashing him took no chances. They spiraled the braided rawhide rope around him from his ankles to his armpits.

They did not enclose Ki's arms while wrapping him in the coils, but now one of the men led the end of the rope through Ki's elbows to pull them together at the back of the post. Then he carried the rope end around Ki's neck and lashed his wrists against his body.

While the Indians were working at binding Ki, they'd talked very little; only an occasional word or two had been exchanged between them. Ki had heard their infrequent remarks, but they spoke in one of the Indian languages with which he was not familiar. Though Ki had been tempted several times to slit his eyelids and get a close look at his captors, he knew they were so close to him that even a flicker of his lids would be seen at once. He kept his eyes closed and allowed his chin to drop as though unconsciousness had relaxed his neck muscles.

At last the Indians finished their task and tugged at the knots of Ki's bonds to give them a final test. One of them spoke a few words in their harsh guttural language and the others responded as briefly. Then Ki heard the soft crunching of their moccasins on the dry ground, the footsteps fading to silence as his captors moved away.

Ki opened his eyes, but did not move for several moments. Then he swiveled his neck to locate the Indians who'd captured him. They were moving up a gentle slope, leading their horses as well as his own mount toward a cluster of tepees that stood at its crest. Ki counted eight of the tall conical tents, dark triangles against the now-reddening sky.

He wondered if there were more tepees hidden from view by the horizon. He continued to watch as the redskins reached the ones he had seen and began to scatter. The men who'd been leading the horses were already out of sight beyond the crest of the rise. Soon the others vanished inside the tepees.

For a moment or so Ki did not move. Then he began to test the suppleness of the strips of leather that bound his wrists. He tried to twist his arms, but as he moved them the bindings bit into his flesh with a cruelly cutting pressure, and he was forced to abandon his efforts. The thongs that held his ankles together were equally unyielding. His struggles had strained Ki's supple muscles to the utmost; he knew that he must rest a few minutes before trying to break free. Letting his head fall forward on his chest, Ki closed his eyes and forced himself to relax as best he could while sagging motionless against the stubborn thongs that held him captive.

"Ki should've been back by now." Jessie frowned. She glanced at the sky, then raised her arm to shield her eyes with the palm of her hand while glancing quickly at the reddening sun. Although it was hanging only a three-finger span above the horizon, it had not yet taken on the deep crimson hue of sunset. She went on, "He's certainly taking a long enough time to do his scouting. I'm beginning to wonder if he might've run into some kind of trouble."

"There's not much trouble for Ki to run into on the little way he'll cover coming around here, Jessie, unless he's met up with some of those outlaws that stole my horses and wrecked my place," Bruce said. "There's no town closer than something like twenty or thirty miles and not much between us and it but rocks and raw dirt."

"You're sure you know where we are, and where the town is?"

"Oh, I'm sure, all right," Bruce replied. "I've scouted over this part of the country enough to know, chasing after strayed horses."

"And the outlaw hideout?" she asked. "You've said that you know just about where it is."

"I've got as close to it as any man in his right mind would want to, unless he's an outlaw hisself." Bruce nodded. "But I don't lay claim to being a hero, Jessie, and I don't figure I'm fool enough to go single-handed against that gang." He waved toward the sheer rock wall of a high plateau outlined against the darkening sky. "I've tracked the rascals to the base of that big mesa yonder, but I never tried to get up to the top of it."

"That's where the outlaws hole up?"

"I'm sure enough to guarantee it. There's a narrow, tricky trail that goes up the back side of it to the top, and I've tracked that bunch to where it starts up."

"But you've never been up the trail yourself?"

"Not even partway," he said emphatically. "Not all by myself. I'd want somebody to cover my back if I was on that zigzag trail I could see winding up its side, because if I was the boss of an outlaw gang I'd have a man guarding it so nobody could sneak up it and surprise me."

"I'd've thought their hideout would be along the riverbank somewhere." Jessie frowned.

"It likely was, a good while back. It's been gov'ment land all along, but I never did fancy it as horse country. Now them fools in the Indian Bureau's filled it up with redskins, and I stay as far away from them ornery rascals as I can."

"And they don't bother you?"

"They ain't so far, but it's a pretty good piece away. And it ain't real good horse country along the river; it's got no graze to speak of." Bruce stopped for a moment before going on, "Anyhow, the Paiutes aren't horse-Indians, like the Comanches. They farm their land, garden truck, corn and such, and a little bit of straggle-boll cotton."

Jessie had been listening only abstractedly, her mind still occupied with Ki's failure to return from a scouting trip that should have taken at most an hour or so to complete.

Now she said, "Unless he had a very good reason to, Ki wouldn't go off on some Indian trail. And I don't see how he could've gotten mixed up about the bunch we're after. The only reason I asked him to go look at the other trail fork again was to make sure the men we're after hadn't split up."

"I reckon they could've done that, maybe trying to keep us from picking up their tracks." Bruce nodded. "But there's such a mixed-up batch of hoofprints on that trail and all alongside it to boot that it's awful hard to figure out which of 'em is the newest and where they was making for."

"All I can think of is that Ki must've found something that bothered him and decided to look into it." Jessie frowned. "It's not like him to waste time, especially when he knows we're waiting."

"Well, Miss Jessie, I don't know Ki near as good as you do," Bruce told her. "But the way I look at it, we've got two or three choices. We can turn back and look for Ki, but I can't think of any trouble he'd get into. Or you can let off that shot signal you mentioned and we'll set here and wait for him. Or we can go on pushing ahead and depend on him to follow our tracks and find us."

A thoughtful look flicked over Jessie's face, but she did not speak for a moment. Then she said, "None of the choices we've got are really satisfactory, but I suppose the best thing we can do is push on. Ki's good at tracking; I'm sure he'll catch up with us."

"That's about the way I feel," Bruce nodded. "But I figure like you do, Ki's going to find us."

"Yes, I'm sure he will," Jessie agreed. "And I certainly don't like the idea of backtracking, because we might just be wasting time. But even if you and I haven't come very far, it'll be dark soon, and Ki won't have any way to find us unless we build a fire."

"Do you figure it'd be a good idea for us to light one out on this level stretch?" Bruce asked. "The outlaws might see it, and once they catch sight of a fire, it ain't likely they'd waste much time sending a man back here to scout around. They'd find out we're looking for 'em and the whole bunch would come at us shooting."

"Yes, I've thought about that," Jessie agreed. "But I'd almost as soon risk it as having Ki lose our trail."

"Which he ain't real likely to do," Bruce assured her. "And if we do have to fight them outlaws, I'd just as lief do it here as in broken country where we've got plenty of cover."

"Let's wait a little while longer, then," Jessie said. "Knowing Ki, I'm positive that he's got a good reason for taking his time coming back, and more than likely he's on his way here by now. All that we need to do is build a little fire that will give him a way to find us in the dark."

"How do you aim to do that without firewood? There's not a tree closer to here than twenty miles."

"There's grass, though," Jessie replied. "And all that Ki would need to come directly to us is just a little gleam. While there's still a few minutes of daylight left, let's grub up some of those bunches of dry grass."

"But if we light any kind of fire the outlaws're bound to see it, too!" Bruce protested. "They'll be down on us in a jiffy if we show them where we are!"

"There's no doubt in my mind about what they'd do if they catch sight of our signals," Jessie replied. "But if we ride on to the bottom of that mesa, they won't be able to see a little fire right at its base. It's getting dark fast, and even if the grass we're going to burn might send up some smoke, it'd be hidden by the dark, too."

"That makes sense," Bruce agreed. "I guess it's a chance we've got to take, anyhow."

"I'm sure it's worth the little risk we'll be taking," Jessie went on. "And even if the outlaws should see the little fire and start down here, we'll certainly know about it. They'd have to come down from the mesa in the dark, and that would make a lot of noise. We'd be sure to hear their horses coming toward us in time to find some kind of cover."

"Well, I guess that's right," Bruce agreed. "Anyways, this dry grass likely won't burn long enough for them to get a fix on it. But if Ki's got off the trail somehow, it oughta help him to find us."

"We'll just move away fast from the fires as soon as we light one," Jessie said. "The grass will only burn a minute or two, but I've got plenty of lucifers in my saddle-bag."

"It looks to me like you've got it all figured out, Jessie," Bruce said.

"Perhaps." Jessie nodded. "But you don't know Ki the way I do. The chances are he might not even need a fire to guide him here, but I don't intend to take any chances. We'll start lighting these little stalks of dry grass just as soon as the sky gets good and dark."

★

Chapter 7

When Ki began trying to break free from his bonds he wasted no time in futile struggling. First he shut out of his mind the painful chafing of the rope that was binding him to the head-high post. Then he closed his eyes and let himself sag, his body totally limp for a few moments. He ignored the strain that his position placed not only on his wrists and forearms, but on the muscles of his neck and back as well.

Ki's wiry sinews finally adjusted to the unaccustomed pressure of the coarse rope. Now he began trying to stretch the loops encircling his wrists by pushing out his chest and flexing his biceps while he twisted his arms to the utmost strain his muscles could endure.

For several minutes Ki exerted himself fully, ignoring both strain and pressure, but in spite of his strength he could feel no hint of slack in the knots even after his repeated efforts. When he realized that he was making no progress, Ki experimented by wriggling and twisting his feet, but he could not bend his knees in order to press them on the hard ground and lever himself upward. The same lack of leverage defeated him when he tried to move his body from side to side or back and forth to loosen the stake from the soil.

None of the efforts that Ki made to free himself eased the

bite of the cruelly cutting rope that lashed his wrists. He kept searching his memory for some other move that he might make that would free him from his bindings, but all that he could think of were moves he had already attempted. Ki tried them again, but with no more effect than the frustration that had marked his first efforts. The rope that entwined his wrists and ankles held him as tightly to the stake as they had when he'd first been tied there.

Ki was still racking his brain, trying to find the elusive leverage that might loosen or even break the rope and open a way to his escape when the soft scraping of moccasins on the hard ground behind him brought his eyes open. He twisted his neck to look.

A young Indian woman stood a few paces away. She was gazing at Ki through the fast-gathering dusk. A puzzled frown on her broad face pulled her thin eyebrows downward until her eyes were barely visible. She wore a shapeless and yellowed white cotton dress that dropped straight from her shoulders and covered her bare legs to mid-calf. Ki spoke before she could.

"Will you help me?" he asked. Ki knew that the woman might not understand English, that his question was a gamble he could lose, but as she came closer to him he could see that the woman did not have the cast of features that marked the men who'd captured him. When he realized that she was not going to reply, Ki tried again.

This time he said, "I'm not asking you to do anything but cut one strand of this rope that is binding my wrists. If you will help me that much, I can manage to do the rest of getting free without help."

For a moment she did not answer, and Ki wondered if she had understood him. Then she shook her head and to Ki's surprise replied in halting and thickly accented English, "If I cut rope the Chiricahuas will kill me, and I do not want to die."

"Neither do I," Ki said quickly. "But who are these Chiricahuas? Another tribe, different from yours?"

Nodding, she went on in a voice that was flat and without emotion, "Chiricahuas kill all people they capture. They will kill you. They might kill me because I talk to you."

"They haven't killed me yet," Ki observed. "And I saw many of your people who live along the river that they have not killed."

"They will," she said. "They will not stop killing until none of my people still live."

"Why would they want to kill your people?"

"It is Chiricahua way. They are of the Apaches in the north, and they are still wild. When they fight, they do not stop until they have killed all their enemies or until all their own fighting men have been killed."

"They don't call your people enemies, then?"

She shook her head. "No. Long ago they did, but not now. They made war on us and beat us and took our land. Now they have killed our fighting men until we have no more than there are fingers on my hands."

"Your people are Paiutes?" Ki asked. He was not especially interested, but by this time the idea had occurred to him that if he could keep the woman talking he might be able not only to gather some useful information, but to arouse her sympathy or her interest in his plight. If he could only do that, maybe he could persuade her to release him.

She shook her head. "We are Dene. Some call us Paiute, but some Apaches are called Paiute, which is not right."

"What's your name?" Ki asked.

"I am called Adelsa. And you?"

"Ki."

Adelsa frowned as she said, "I have never heard of a name like this among any of the people—"

Ki broke in quickly. He said, "Names do not matter. You have not heard of one like mine because my people live far away. But we can wait until later to talk of this. You said that even though they belong to your own tribe these Chiricahuas kill your men. Why are they your enemies?"

"Only the Chiricahuas can tell you, and they say nothing. But only a few of our men still live. Some dress like women; some hide during daylight and come out only at night. A few of them do not come out of their tepees at all."

"Don't the Indians who kill your men kill women, too?"

Adelsa shook her head. "They need us to make babies. They have only a few women of their own tribe. They take our babies from us and make them Chiricahuas."

"How did the Chiricahuas get here?" Ki asked.

"A long time ago the soldiers brought them here, when the white settlers to the east and the north wanted the Chiricahuas' hunting grounds to make farms on. While the soldiers stayed, the Chiricahuas made no trouble. They had learned that the soldiers had better guns than theirs."

Adelsa stopped talking and Ki asked, "Your people had no guns?"

"We are not a fighting people, Ki," she answered. "We of the Dene have always been peaceful. When the soldiers left, the Chiricahuas soon went back to their old ways of killing. Soon they had killed all our young fighting men, only the old ones were left, and our people were driven away from our land. Now there are not many of us left. There are not enough young men and young women to make babies. We live in the river canyon now."

"Because your people are afraid of them?"

"Only fools do not fear the Chiricahuas. I say again, they are Apaches of the north, still wild."

"You said your people are Dene," Ki frowned. "Isn't that the same as Paiute?"

"Some call us Paiute, some say we are Apache, but this is wrong. True Paiute and Apache people are still wild. We Dene are peaceful. We lived here in this place until the soldiers brought the Chiricahuas from lands the whites wanted."

"You speak very good English." Ki frowned. "Did you learn it from the soldiers?"

"No. When my people lived peacefully here there were

holy men of the whites who taught us their language. But the Chiricahuas killed them, just as they did our people."

"You owe these Chiricahuas nothing, then," Ki said. "Now I will ask you again. Cut this rope, so I can be free."

As she'd done earlier, Adelsa shook her head. "I cannot." She looked around as though she was expecting to see a band of wild Indians somewhere close by as she went on, "The Chiricahuas would kill me."

"They wouldn't know it was you. They're in those tepees over there," Ki broke in, bending his head in the direction of the shadowed triangles silhouetted against the fast-deepening blue of the western sky. "They're not likely to see us."

For a long moment Adelsa said nothing, but continued to scan the area around them. Turning back to Ki, she said hesitatingly, "You are not of our people, but you are not of the white man's kind. What your tribe?"

"I have no tribe."

"How can this be? All people must have a tribe."

"My people live far away, beyond the western sea," Ki explained. "Do you know where the great sea is?"

She shook her head as she replied, "I have heard of the big water, but I have never seen it." After a moment she went on, "But if you are from so far away, why are the Chiricahuas your enemies?"

"They are—" Ki stopped as he realized the futility of trying to explain his situation. He went on, "It would take a very long time for me to tell you. But they are my enemies, just as they are enemies of your people. Before I could finish telling you why, they might come back. Then we will have lost our chance to escape them."

"No," Adelsa said. "They will not come out of their tepees until it is almost time for the sun to rise."

"How can you be sure?"

"It is the Chiricahua way. They do not like darkness. When they have captured an enemy they stay at night in their medicine tepees, dancing and singing their killing songs."

77

"How long do they dance and sing?" Ki asked her.

"Until the sky begins to light they do nothing but sing. What they do in their tepees is their way of getting ready to come here and make their death dance."

"Tell me about their death dance," Ki suggested. "How long do they dance it?"

"Before the sun comes up, but after the sky is bright, they start the dance. When the sun first shows they begin to cut with their knives. After the sun has climbed above the earth they sheathe the knives and use their tomahawks. They do not stop dancing when the man on the stake dies. They cut with their tomahawks until he is only bones. I have seen this. I know what they do."

"Then you know my story is true, and that I will die when they come back," Ki said. "If you would only help me get free from—"

Adelsa broke in before he could finish. "No! If I help you, the Chiricahuas would kill me, too!"

"How would they know?" he asked. "There are none of them here now to see you."

"They would know," she replied. "Chiricahuas can read the signs of footprints in the dirt."

"If you cut me free, we can leave together and you can walk ahead of me," Ki suggested. "I will follow you and wipe out your prints and mine, too."

"You do not know the Chiricahuas," Adelsa replied. Again Ki could hear fear in her voice. "They can see prints in the earth even when someone tries to hide them."

"I've told you, I'll follow you and wipe out our footprints, or I'll carry you on my back when we leave," Ki said.

Again Adelsa shook her head. Then she repeated, "They would know. You could not wipe out all the footprints I made when I was coming here. They would see them and if they saw no footprints leaving they would know you carried me."

"And you'll let them kill me?" Ki asked. "You won't help me get away?"

78

"I cannot!" Her voice echoed fearfully as she went on. "I have great fear of the Chiricahuas! They kill our people just as they do one of their horses when it does not please them!"

"We will only need to get to my horse," Ki said. "When the Chiricahuas went to their tepees, they took it with them. I'll get it back while they're in their tepees; then both of us can ride it and you will leave no tracks for them to follow."

"Chiricahuas are good trackers," Adelsa said slowly. "They can tell when two people ride the same horse."

In spite of her negative reply, Ki was sure that he heard the first sign of yielding in Adelsa's voice. He said, "When we get to your tepee you can stay and I'll ride on away from it. The Chiricahuas will follow me. They won't stop to bother you."

"You are sure you can do this?" she asked.

Putting into his voice all the confidence he could muster, Ki said, "I've made false trails before. It will be very easy for me to make another one."

"But will you come back to my house and stay to fight the Chiricahuas if they find out I have helped you?"

"Of course," he assured her. "Even without the gun I have on my horse I still have weapons to use against them."

After a moment of brow-furrowed silence Adelsa nodded and said, "I will untie you. But you must promise to stay with me until I am sure the Chiricahuas will not kill me."

"I will stay as long as there's a need to fight them," Ki promised.

Nodding, Adelsa slid a sheathed knife from the bosom of her dress. Pulling it from its sheath, she began cutting Ki's bonds. As they fell, he stepped away from the tall post and began rubbing his hands to restore their feeling.

"We must go quickly," she urged. "If the Chiricahuas hear us, they will kill us!"

Ki was pulling his loose jacket about him to shield himself against the small recurring ripples of cold air. He stopped short as his hand encountered the leather case holding his *shuriken* that he'd put in the jacket's pocket earlier in the day when he waded into the river.

Seeing Ki's face Adelsa asked, "Is something wrong?"

Shaking his head, Ki replied, "No. But I've just found that when the Chiricahuas took my weapons they didn't strip me completely."

"Will your weapons be better than theirs?" She frowned.

"Perhaps no better, but they still serve me well," Ki assured her. Knowing that he was not completely weaponless boosted his spirits. He went on, "Let's go to the tepees where the Chiricahuas are doing whatever it is they do before they kill one of their prisoners. If what you've told me is true, they won't pay a great deal of attention to anything outside of their tepees."

"This is a true thing," Adelsa agreed.

"Then there's a pretty good chance for us to ride away from here without them knowing we've escaped," Ki said. "Come on. This may be the only chance we'll have."

"Something must have happened to Ki," Jessie said to Bruce. "He'd've been back long before now from doing such a simple job. And it's not as though he's a tenderfoot who'd get lost in the dark."

"I've been wondering myself when he'll get back," Bruce agreed. Now that Jessie had broached the subject of Ki's long unexplained absence he felt free to admit the worried thoughts that had been prodding his own mind. "I just didn't want to bother you by saying anything."

"I'm not exactly bothered," Jessie went on. "Ki can take care of himself quite well."

Bruce's response came quickly. He said, "I never meant to say he couldn't, even if it's in country like this, that's strange to him just like it is to me and you. But it's plumb dark now, and that sorta puts us between a rock and a hard place. I'm afraid the horse thieves up on that mesa yonder are going to see these fires we've been lighting."

"Do you think it'll spook them all that badly?" Jessie asked. "They'd just take it for granted that we're some travelers passing through."

"Well, maybe I'm just still edgy on account of what they did to my little horse ranch," Bruce agreed. "So let's take a chance and light another fire. Even if they was to see it, and they took a notion to come find out about us, it'd take a while for 'em to get here. And for all we know, Ki might not be too far off, looking for us."

"I've been thinking about that, too, so let's take our chances on the outlaws," Jessie agreed. "Go ahead and light the fire, Bruce. Even if it might stir the outlaws out, we've got to think first about helping Ki."

When Ki turned and started toward the tepees, Adelsa exclaimed, "Wait! We must go away from the Chiricahuas, not closer to them!"

"No," Ki replied, turning back to face her. "We can't go on foot and leave their horses for them. If we do, they can ride after us and they will be moving faster than we can."

"But I have no horse!" Adelsa protested.

"You will have," Ki promised. "I'll take my horse and one of theirs for you to ride, then I'll scatter the rest of them so the Chiricahuas can't chase after us."

"Won't they hear us if we get close to their tepees?"

"I can move silently," Ki assured her.

Adelsa was silent for a moment. Then she nodded and said, "I will do as you say. Tell me what you wish me to do."

"Walk beside me until I stop," Ki told her. "Do nothing until I tell you to. I'll get my horse and one for you. We'll lead them until we're sure the Chiricahuas won't hear us when we mount them and start away. If we're lucky, they won't be able to follow us in the darkness."

"I will do as you say," Adelsa promised.

"Good," Ki replied. "Now let's not waste any more time. Just remember what I've told you and we may be able to get away."

★

Chapter 8

Ki had been walking up the long stretch of gently rising ground toward the tepees for several minutes before he realized that Adelsa was always a half pace behind him. He began stopping now and then to allow her to come abreast of him, but each time that he stopped, Adelsa also halted.

After he'd stopped for the third time, Ki realized belatedly that she was observing the age-old Indian custom that required women to remain a respectful step or two behind any man with whom she might be walking. At the same time, Ki understood now that no matter how slowly or how fast he might walk, and regardless of how frequently he halted, Adelsa would continue to honor the traditions and customs of her people. After that he did not stop, but continued to advance steadily.

They reached a point where the bases as well as the tops of the tepees became visible, and now they could hear the muffled thunks of slowly spaced drumbeats and the sharper sound of atonal chanting coming from them. At times one man's voice would rise above the others in a chilling shriek that quavered and hung in the air for what seemed to be a very long time before fading away.

"Do you know the song they are singing?" Ki asked as he

and Adelsa forged steadily ahead. "To me, it sounds like an unhappy one."

"It is the Chiricahuas killing song," she told him. "The one they sing when they capture enemies and bring them here to kill with many little knife cuts."

"They're singing for me, then," Ki observed. "What will they do when they don't find me still tied to the stake?"

"They will be very angry," she replied soberly. "They think that to let a prisoner escape makes them small. If they catch you now, they will not sing any more. They will kill you slowly, the death of a thousand knife cuts. It will take you a very long time to die."

"All the more reason for us to hurry, then," Ki said. "We'd better move as fast as we can to get to the horses and be on our way before they come out of their tepees."

In the deep gloom of the moonless night the conical outlines of the shelters appeared to recede as Ki and Adelsa advanced. Then as they drew closer the illusions of distances resolved themselves. Soon the tepees were only a short distance, twenty or thirty paces, ahead of them. Now the harsh voices of the singers had grown much louder.

Beyond the tepees, on a gentle downslope, Ki and Adelsa could glimpse the Chiricahuas' horses. The animals were not confined or tethered. They were moving around slowly as they sought the occasional grassy spots that showed here and there in patches of a darker hue than that of the hard, rocky barren soil.

Ki and Adelsa were passing the tepees now. Turning to her, Ki tapped his chest with his forefinger and pointed to the horses. Then he lowered his hand palm-down, its fingers spread, and raised it to point to her. Adelsa understood his gesture and shook her head.

"No," she said, keeping her voice low. "Please, let me stay with you, Ki. I am afraid one of the Chiricahuas might come out of a tepee. He would see me and—" Her voice trailed off into silence.

Ki hesitated for only a moment. He could not bring himself to refuse. He nodded, and with Adelsa continuing to follow a pace or two behind him, he began altering his course. Now he moved to make a wide semicircle away from the tepees in order to avoid the danger of being seen or heard by the men inside them.

As they advanced, Ki blinked his eyes often, squeezing his eyelids together to improve his night vision. Then he started looking for his own horse. For a few moments he flicked his eyes across the dozen or more steeds that were ambling around slowly with their heads down, seeking the sparse graze that was offered by the barren land.

Sooner than he'd hoped, Ki caught sight of his mount. It was still saddled and its size, markedly bigger than the small Indian ponies, together with the high horn and cantle of its saddle, set it apart from the horses belonging to the Indians. Gesturing for Adelsa to follow him, Ki began weaving between the dozen or so slowly ambling horses that belonged to the Chiricahuas.

When they'd gotten within a few paces of his horse, Ki glanced around at the animals nearest him. There was little to choose between them, and he grabbed for the reins of the one he could reach most easily. Extending his free hand to Adelsa, Ki helped her clamber onto the back of the Indian horse. Then he led the pony to within a step of his own mount.

"You ride in front of me," he told her. "You know the shortest way to reach your house much better than I do. Don't try to go fast. Just let your horse walk."

"I understand that we must make little noise," she said. "But what if the Chiricahuas—"

"They won't know we're gone unless we disturb their horses and start them whinneying and stamping around," Ki broke in. "And I'm sure we can find a place to hide our horses close to wherever your house is. When the Chiricahuas start trying to find me, they'll look for the horses first. Is there a good place to hide them near your house?"

"I can hide them well," Adelsa nodded. "But not close

to my house. There are not many places here in the river canyon where a horse can be hidden."

"All that we need is a place where the horses won't be seen easily, but one that we can get get to quickly," Ki said. "I'm sure you'll find the best place to put them. Now there's only one thing more. If the Chiricahuas find out that I've gotten away from them before we're out of sight, they'll start after us at once. If they do, I'll hold them off as best I can while you ride on and find a place to hide."

"But you can't—" she began.

Ki broke in, his voice stern. "Yes, I can! I have my rifle again, and other weapons in my saddlebags. Now, let's get away from here as quickly as possible, before they stop singing and dancing and come out of the tepees."

"We should hurry, then," she said.

"Just as quickly as we can," Ki agreed. "Oh, one thing more. Unless the Chiricahuas do come out, don't let your horse go faster than a walk while you're leading the way. You know the trail. I don't."

Adelsa reined her horse around and toed it ahead. Ki followed her, twisting in his saddle now and then to look back and be sure that the Indians in the tepee were still inside it carrying on their ceremonies.

As they rode, Ki reached behind him into his saddlebags, fumbling to find the leather cases in which he carried his supply of *shuriken*. At last his fingers encountered one of the cases, and he could tell by its weight that it was full of the throwing-blades. While still controlling the reins of his horse, Ki managed to strap the case on his left arm, then reached back to find a second case, which he strapped on above the first.

Their slow progress across the level ground ended abruptly at the base of the sinuous line of towering stone. Adelsa turned her horse to ride along its base. Ki followed her closely until they reached the narrow cleft that marked the passageway to the river trail. Adelsa looked over her shoulder at Ki and gestured toward the black gap. She was reining her horse toward it when behind them a loud shout sounded. It was followed almost at once by a babble of confused yelling.

Twisting in her saddle to face Ki, Adelsa exclaimed, "The Chiricahuas!"

"Yes, they must have found that I've gotten free," Ki said. "Let's hope we'll be out of here and on our way before they can get mounted and begin chasing us. We've got to find a hiding place as fast as we can."

"There's a trail to the river just past the place where we will go out of the gap, but there is no place along it where we can hide," she told him.

"Is the trail narrow?"

"Yes. It goes through a split in the big stones."

"Then let's get on it," Ki told her. "The sooner we reach the river, the better. Go on. I'll stay right behind you."

Adelsa dug her heels into the flanks of her horse, and with Ki riding close behind her, she started at a gallop toward the box canyon's high wall. She did not try to check her horse as they approached the high stone buttress. At the last moment, when Ki thought that she was going to ride into the face of the towering cliff, Adelsa reined aside sharply and led him into a narrow gap, barely wide enough for a horse and rider to enter.

For a short distance the gap ran almost straight; then it appeared to be closing. Still Adelsa gave no sign that she intended to rein in. A few yards from the seemingly solid granite formation, she yanked at the reins and disappeared. Ki was following as closely as possible now, and as he approached the place where Adelsa had vanished, he could see the curve in the narrow passage. Straining his eyes, he managed to keep his horse in the center of the path, where there was the least danger that a protruding section of the walls would scrape him out of the saddle.

Suddenly a dim slit of light appeared; then a black shadow blocked it out. Ki was just beginning to tighten his reins when the dim light reappeared and he realized that Adelsa had reached the end of the passageway. Within a few more moments he also rode out of the deep shadows of the split, and ahead he saw the glint of stars reflected from the surface of the river. Then he was outside of the gap and on the riverbank. Adelsa had reined in and was waiting for him on the narrow strip between the towering stone cliff and the dancing gleams of starshine on the water's dark surface.

"In my house, I think we will be safe," she told Ki as he reined in beside her. "The Chiricahuas will not start to follow us at once. They cannot see our trail in the dark, and there are many places where the trail above the river valley goes over rocks that will not show the prints of our horses' hooves."

"I've been worried about the horses," Ki said. "Hiding one is not easy. Do you know of a place near your house where the Chiricahuas won't be likely to find them?"

"Near my house there is a deep crevice in the wall of the valley," she replied. "I do not know whether we can put the horses in there, but we can try."

"We'll try, then," Ki told her. "And if we can hide the horses there, I'll stay with you in your house. We need some time to decide what we must do next."

"We don't have a great deal of choice, Bruce," Jessie said as she looked at the brightening strip of before-sunrise dawn moving slowly upward from the black horizon and beginning to lighten the sky. "We'll just have to let the horse thieves wait while we turn back and try to find Ki."

"My guess is that he's run into some kind of trouble." Bruce frowned. "It's sure not like Ki to lollygag around when he's heading for someplace."

"Yes." Jessie nodded. "What's bothering me now is that we might've waited too long, but there's no point in regretting a lost opportunity."

"I got to agree with you, Miss Jessie," Bruce said. "But what's got me buffaloed is where he could've got off to. It just ain't Ki's way not to finish up a little job like you asked him to do and then not come back right away."

"No, Ki's always prompt," she replied. "But I'm sure that somewhere along the trail we've been following or even as far back as the river, he'll have managed to leave some sort of sign for us. I haven't any idea what it could be, but knowing Ki, even if he's in trouble he'll have worked out a way to give us a trail to follow."

"If he did, we'll find it," Bruce assured her. "Now I'll go saddle up and we can start soon as we have a bite of breakfast."

Before Jessie could say anything more, Bruce headed for their horses. Jessie watched him for a moment as he started saddling them; then she turned her attention to rolling up their blankets and replacing in their saddlebags the small bits and pieces of gear they'd taken out to cook supper the evening before. As she was finishing her chores, Bruce returned, leading the horses. He looked at her and frowned.

"Jessie, hadn't we better eat a bite of breakfast before we start out?" he asked.

"Well, we don't exactly have a restaurant with us," Jessie replied. "But right now getting started to look for Ki is more important than eating. Let's just take a handful of soda crackers out of the victuals pack and eat while we're riding."

"If dry crackers are good enough for you, I guess they're good enough for me." Bruce nodded.

Jessie opened the pack she'd just finished rolling and found the tall tin box that held crackers and the remains of a loaf of bread. She held it out to Bruce, who stuffed a handful of the big square crackers into his shirt pocket. Then Jessie filled one of her shirt pockets, remade the pack, and lashed it on her mount with saddle strings. When Bruce saw her step up to her horse and slip a foot into the stirrup, he mounted his own nag. Keeping together, they started along the trail back to the river canyon.

They'd ridden across the level featureless expanse of gently rolling prairie for what seemed to Jessie to be a very short time when they reached the sharp decline that led to the river canyon. Jessie reined in and Bruce pulled up beside her.

"Did you see something up ahead?" he asked.

She shook her head as she replied, "No. I just thought this might be a good place for us to fan out and see if we can pick up Ki's trail. I've been looking for the hoofprints that his horse must've left when he came back this way, but so far I haven't seen any."

"No more have I," Bruce agreed. "But if I'd had to come back this way, I'd've been cutting a straight line down that long slope we just passed over instead of winding around on this zigzagging trail like we did yesterday."

"Maybe I'm a little bit too worried to think straight," Jessie said. "It just didn't occur to me that Ki could've done anything but follow the trail, the way we did going upslope. Perhaps the smart thing for us to do is to fan out, Bruce. You go right and I'll go left, and we'll see if we have better luck than we've had so far."

With a nod of agreement, Bruce reined away from the trail on the right-hand side and started cutting across the slope. Jessie turned in the opposite direction. She watched the ground carefully, holding her horse to a walk as she scanned the ground. Jessie saw nothing helpful. At no place in the sparse grasses that grew between rock outcrops in the thin layer of crusted brown soil did the ground show signs of having been disturbed by a horse's hooves.

A shout from Bruce reached Jessie's ears. She turned to see him standing up in his stirrups, waving at her. She reined around and toed her horse to a faster gait as she hurried to rejoin him.

"I think I've found what we're looking for," Bruce said when Jessie reached his side. "I'll bet my bottom dollar that I've found Ki's tracks."

"I certainly hope you have," she told him as she swiveled to look at the crescentlike hoofprints. "Because I didn't see a thing in the direction I took."

"He must've cut off the trail we followed coming up

here," Bruce went on. "But just look right yonder and you'll see where a horse slanted across that little dip to get on the main trail to the river. Ki's horse is about the only one that could've left those prints. I'd say he figured just like I would, that he'd make better time going that way."

Jessie swiveled in her saddle to look where Bruce pointed. Then she nodded her agreement as she replied, "I'm sure you're right. Let's see if we can follow those hoofprints."

"I haven't heard anything but the wind since we stopped," Ki said to Adelsa. "I can't believe that we've gotten away from the Chiricahuas so easily."

"We have been lucky." She smiled.

It was the first time that Ki had seen any expression but fear or sober thought on her face. He said, "Perhaps we can hold onto our streak of luck. Do you know of a place where we can hide? Somewhere close by, that we can get to until we're sure the Chiricahuas have turned back?"

"There are only a few places the Chiricahuas do not go. One is our village. It is on the trail that leads—"

Ki broke in, "You don't need to go on, Adelsa. I'm sure I've seen the place you're thinking of. Isn't it the little settlement your people have made along the river?"

"Yes, of course," she replied. "You'd have ridden through it on the way to the Chiricahuas—"

Ki broke in, "I didn't ride through it. They carried me through it like I was a deer or some other kind of animal. All I got was an upside-down look. But most of the houses I got a glimpse of didn't look like they'd be solid enough to hide much of anything."

"They would not be," she agreed. "But if you have on the clothes such as our men wear, and do nothing to make them look at you, the Chiricahuas would take you for one of us."

"I think you're right," Ki agreed. "But the horses—"

Adelsa interrupted him. She said, "We will stop and hide them on the way, somewhere close to my house. I know of

91

places where they can be hidden."

"Then let's hurry and get there," Ki suggested. "If we're lucky, the Chiricahuas will be scattered out along the river trail, and any other trail they might think we've taken. You know the canyon better than I do, so you ride ahead of me."

With a quick nod, Adelsa reined her horse around. Ki let her start and followed close behind her. The sky was bright now with the sun's first rising rays, but the wide, high-walled canyon through which the river ran was in its period of transition from night to day. The side the trail ran along was still bathed in deep shadow, but it was obvious to Ki that Adelsa had a destination in mind, for she did not look from right to left or twist in her saddle to make sure that he was following.

They'd covered a substantial distance, and the sunlight was touching the ragged stone tips of the canyon wall on the opposite side of the river before Adelsa twisted in her saddle and gestured for Ki to rein in. She brought her horse to a stop at the same time. She swung out of her saddle and walked back to Ki, who was following her lead and dismounting.

"We must lead our horses from here," she told him. "And hide our trail as we go. Just ahead of us there is a wide, deep crack in the river canyon wall. It is big enough to hide our horses in. My friend's house isn't far. She'll lend you some of her husband's clothes."

Ki had been examining the canyon ahead while Adelsa talked. As she started leading the horses along the trail, Ki pointed to a ragged clump of weeds that was growing out of one of the dirt-filled cracks in the canyon wall.

"I'll pull some of this brush and walk behind you, sweeping away the prints we'll leave," he said. "If our luck is good, the Chiricahuas will gallop right on by. Even if they can figure out what we've done, they'll be delayed long enough to give us a better chance of getting away safely."

Adelsa was already moving ahead, leading the horses. Ki pulled a clump of dry brush from one of the cracks in the wall. He began backing away, brushing the surface of the trail. It was a slow, painstaking job, and by the time he'd reached the crevice, Adelsa was just coming back onto the trail.

"We'd better hurry now," she said. "If we don't waste our time we just might be lucky enough to be safe in my house before the Chiricahuas get here."

★

Chapter 9

"How much further do we have to go?" Ki asked Adelsa. He waved a hand at the sky, where the rim of the sun was now showing at the horizon, though a semidarkness still lay on the trail. Gesturing toward the trail they'd been moving along since hiding their horses, he went on, "It seems to me we've been walking for quite a while."

"Perhaps my house is further than you had thought it would be," she replied. "But we will reach it very soon, now. First we must stop at the house of the friend I told you of. It's just beyond that big rock that you see sticking out of the cliff directly ahead."

"It does seem to me that we've traveled a long while," Ki admitted. "But the last time I went over this trail I wasn't thinking too much about looking for landmarks. I was being carried in the other direction, and I know now how a market calf must feel on the way to the slaughter pen."

"That was after the Chiricahuas had first captured you?"

"Yes. I couldn't see much except the ground and the men who were carrying me. You see, they were holding me upside down."

"Upside down?" Adelsa frowned.

"My face was always upside-down," Ki explained. "Every

time I twisted my neck trying to look for landmarks they'd start shaking me. About the only thing I got a really good look at was the dirt of the trail and the rocks beside it."

"But this thing has already happened, Ki. You do not need to think about it now," she said. Raising her arm, Adelsa pointed ahead, where a vee of deep blue showed a curve in the trail. "We must stop first at the house that we will soon see just past that bend."

"That's where the friend you mentioned lives? The one you said will lend me some clothing for disguise?"

"Yes. My house is still a little bit further away. But we must stop for a small time where my good friends live. I'm sure they will lend you the clothes you must wear to be safe here."

"Do you think that's really necessary?" Ki frowned. "Once we're indoors, it isn't likely we'll be going outside again until it's dark. And we haven't seen or heard any of the Chiricahuas since we got away from them."

Adelsa shook her head as she said, "There is little time of darkness left, Ki. By the time we get to my friend's house the sun will be bright. And I know the ways of the Chiricahuas. You are their enemy, and because I have helped you escape, I am now their enemy, too. When they allow an enemy to escape from them, they lose much face. Do you understand what face means?"

"Quite well." Ki nodded. "Every Indian tribe feels that it's disgraced when one of its enemies gets the best of its fighting men."

"Yes," Adelsa agreed. "And they have much anger when they lose face. If we were not their enemies before, we are now. I'm sure that their fighting men have found our trail by now and are not too far behind us."

"If they're like most of the Indians I know about, they're not likely to give up and turn back."

"It would not be like them to give up," she agreed. "If they see you as you are now, they would recognize you at once. We would be very foolish to take that chance."

"That's not really what I've been thinking about," Ki told her. "We've been too busy for me to tell you the whole story of why my friends and I have come here."

"Then, tell me now."

"You already know that I'm not traveling alone, Adelsa. I left the people I'm with yesterday evening, and I should have been back with them long ago. I'm sure they'll be coming to look for me. They could be in real danger, not knowing about the Chiricahuas. I need to find them as soon as I can so they'll know that I'm all right."

"You know where they are?" She frowned.

"Yes, of course," Ki told her. He pointed to the imposing bulk of the distant mesa that had just come into sight and was outlined against the steadily brightening sky as they rounded the curve in the trail. Then he went on, "Unless my friends have gotten worried and started out to look for me, they're there, waiting for me to get back."

"Are they on that first big mesa, or the next one?"

"I can only see one now, and I'm sure it's the one we saw from the trail we were following here," Ki replied. "Is there another big mesa close by?"

"There are three big ones," Adelsa replied. "You cannot see the other two from here or from the flatland. The first one is the biggest of the three. The other two behind it are smaller and not as high."

"Do you know anything about those three mesas, Adelsa? Is there a ranch on any of them?"

She shook her head. "This is something I do not know. But look ahead of us, Ki, along the trail. My house is just beyond that one we're coming to now, where we'll stop to borrow the clothes you must have."

Ki turned his eyes to the trail in front of them. The house that Adelsa had indicated to be their stopping place was one of the fragile-looking structures he'd glimpsed when the Chiricahuas were carrying him from the river to their tepees.

It was roughly dome-shaped, woven of large twigs mixed

with the thick, wiry stems of the high, sturdy prairie grasses that grew in big patches on the level land across the riverbed. The portion of the dwelling that he could see was not broken by windows or a door.

As though she was reading Ki's mind, Adelsa said, "The doors of our houses are always on the side away from the trail. We build them that way so that if the Chiricahuas come looking for us they cannot burst through a door and trap us. With our door in the back, we will have time to run and hide before they can catch us inside."

Ki nodded as Adelsa began slanting across the wide path, heading for the house she'd pointed out. She led him around the little hovel before calling in a language he did not understand. A woman's voice answered her call. In a moment she came out of the hut, stooping to pass through the low open arch that served as a doorway. When she stood erect again outside the hut she addressed Adelsa, a few quick guttural remarks.

Adelsa replied with a long choppy rattle of short, harshly accented words that Ki did not even make an effort to understand. She and the woman spoke for a moment in their unintelligible tongue. Then Adelsa turned to Ki.

"Sega, my friend here, will lend you some of her man's clothes. Then you will look like the rest of us and if you are careful the Chiricahuas will pay you no attention."

Turning back to Sega, Adelsa had another quick exchange with her before the woman nodded and returned to the house. After a few moments she returned, one arm draped with folds of white cloth.

As Sega held up the cloth and shook it out, Ki recognized it as one of the short robes he'd seen on the few Paiute men he'd glimpsed when he was being carried by his Chiricahua captors. Adelsa and Sega were speaking again now, but their conversation lasted only a moment or two. Then Adelsa gestured toward Ki. Sega stepped to his side and handed Ki the garment.

"Take it," Adelsa told him. "It is what you must wear as

long as there's any danger that one of the Chiricahuas might get even a quick glimpse of you."

Ki was already shaking out the robe. He held it up to his shoulders, and saw that it would cover him to the knees. Then he turned to Adelsa to ask, "Should I put this on now?"

"Whatever you wish." She shrugged. "But we will not go very far. My house is only a small distance, a few steps down the trail and on its other side, against the cliff."

"Just the same, I think it might be wise for me to put it on now," Ki told her. "I'll roll up the legs of my trousers so I'll look bare-legged. Then if the Chiricahuas should get here, they won't be likely to recognize me."

Adelsa nodded and turned back to Sega. They exchanged a few quick words in their own language, and by the time Adelsa faced Ki again, he'd rolled up his trouser legs and pulled the oversized shirtlike garment over his head. It might have been a twin to the similar attire that he had glimpsed on the Paiute men while the Chiricahuas were carrying him to their village.

Made of loosely woven off-white cotton fabric stitched to create a stubby cylinder, the Paiute garb had been sewn in tucks at the shoulders to create sleeveless openings for his arms and his head. The loosely hemmed bottom dropped to Ki's knees, and capacious patch pockets had been stitched on just below what would have been a waistline if the garment had boasted such a refinement. Putting it on changed Ki's appearance completely.

"Now you look enough like one of our Dene men to keep from attracting any special attention." Adelsa smiled.

"Perhaps so," Ki told her. "But it's going to take me a little while to get used to it. And I'll have to wear my *shuriken* cases like bracelets or armlets so I can get to them quickly if I need to."

"It's just what you need to deceive the Chiricahuas," Adelsa said. Turning to the Paiute woman, she addressed her again. Sega nodded and smiled. Adelsa turned back to Ki and went

99

on. "Sega says you look like one of our men, so perhaps our enemies won't be quick to recognize you. But instead of standing here, we'd better move along to my house. Until now we have been very lucky, but I'm sure the Chiricahuas have already started to look for us, and they may be here at any minute."

"I wish we had a better idea about exactly where Ki went when he came back here yesterday." Jessie frowned. "It's getting late, and all the looking we've done hasn't helped us much. His trail just seems to stop here at the riverbank."

"When you get just a little ways away from the river, this ground's almost as hard as rock," Bruce said. "It's sure mighty deceitful when you're trying to tell which hoofprints is the ones you're looking for."

"There are certainly enough prints right on the riverbank here to make some pretty good guesses," Jessie went on. "And we're sure now of one thing. Ki got this far on his way back to join us. But where could he have gone from here?"

"Well, there's enough prints right here on the riverbank so we can be pretty sure he didn't leave here by hisself," Bruce told her.

"Yes," Jessie agreed. "And it's easy enough to see that he was by himself on that trail we picked up further on along the river."

"Now, I'd guess that he got into some sort of fracas right along in here." Bruce frowned as he examined the pocked ground. "And it had to be with some sort of Indians, because there's just one set of prints of a shoed horse, and that's Ki's. But then you can see how his horse's hoofprints just got swallowed up by all these others."

"Both of us agree on that." Jessie nodded. "And even if I have trouble making myself believe it, Ki either went along with the Indians, or—" She stopped short, as though she was reluctant to carry her reasoning to a conclusion.

"Or they yanked him off his horse and toted him whether

he wanted to go or not," Bruce finished for her.

Jessie nodded. Her face was very sober. At last she said, "We'll just have to follow these hoofprints wherever they lead us, Bruce."

"There isn't any difference between my house and the others around here," Adelsa said.

As she spoke she gestured toward a hut that might well have been a twin to those scattered around it. Like the hut where they'd stopped for Ki's disguising clothes, the little structure was made of reeds woven into a dome. It had a pair of widely spaced slits in the wall. They were only as broad as a man's hand, and the breaks they created were not visible at a glance. As Ki passed the first one, he could see that at the back the reeds from which the wall had been woven were slanted inward across the opening in a manner that made it virtually impossible for anyone standing outside to peer into the interior.

"Your people build well with what you have to work with," Ki told Adelsa as he followed her inside.

"We've learned to do with very little," she replied, gesturing toward the circular area the hut enclosed. It was not quite bare, but gave the appearance of being totally without furnishings. "After the Chiricahuas drove us away from our land where they now have their tepees, we spent many years learning to live with what we could find along the river valley."

Then, as Ki's eyes adjusted to the dimness, he could see a pair of stools at one side of the room, a small table close to the wall behind them. A tier of narrow shelves hugged the wall a few steps away from the table. Pottery vessels stood on them. On the opposite side of the circular room there was a quite passable bed. It was wide, but rose only shin-high; a tousle of blankets covered it, bulging above some sort of mattress. Near one of the bed's ends a short branch had been fixed to the wall. On it hung two or three dresses similar to the one Adelsa was wearing.

"We of the Dene own little but our pride," Adelsa told Ki. "It was not this way before we were driven from the land the Chiricahuas took from us."

"Why didn't you fight them?" Ki asked.

"Our old men who know such things have told us that we tried to fight. They say we did not have enough guns, the bows and arrows of our fighters could not match our enemies' rifles. And there were no men of the Indian Bureau here when the fighting began. After a long time, when they did come here and listen to our story, they said that too many of our men had been killed for us to think of holding our land if the Chiricahuas took it back. They told us that it was too late to change things."

"So, that's how your people came to be scattered out along the riverbank?"

"Yes. But now that we are here and safe, we waste time when we should be resting, Ki. The bed is waiting, but take off your trousers so that if the Chiricahuas do come here they will not take you for anything except one of us."

Though Adelsa's invitation surprised Ki, her logic made sense. He stripped off his trousers and laid them aside, then loosed the straps of the cases of *shuriken* on his arms and put them on the floor beside the bed. Pulling the long loose cotton robe around himself, he stretched out on the bed. Adelsa surprised him again by lying down beside him.

"I wake easily," she said. "If the Chiricahuas come near, I will hear their horses' hooves and wake you."

Already half-asleep after his exertions of the night, Ki nodded as he replied, "I wake easily, too. I'm sure we won't be caught napping." Then he closed his eyes and was asleep within a few moments.

Ki did not know how long he'd been asleep when the soft tentative touch of Adelsa's fingers on his *cache-sex* woke him. The light in the little hut was not as bright as it had been, and he turned his head to look at her. Adelsa was propped up on an elbow, her hand hovering over his crotch.

She glanced at Ki and their eyes locked.

"You've slept long enough to be refreshed," she said. "And I didn't want to wait any longer. I have an itching, Ki. Will you do what I must have to end it?"

As Adelsa spoke, she rose to a sitting position. She reached down to grasp the hem of her dress and pull it over her head. She wore nothing underneath it. Ki watched the swaying of her full breasts as she tossed the garment to the floor.

Adelsa's outright suggestion and her movements had caught Ki unawares. He was surprised, but she was not the first woman to make the same suggestion. Lifting himself to lean on an elbow, Ki gazed at Adelsa's nude body. The light bronze of her smooth skin set off her sparse coal-black pubic brush, and the budded rosettes of her generous breasts were not pink, but a darker bronze than her skin.

As he looked at her, Ki was very much aware of his beginning erection, for the sight of Adelsa's naked body had reminded him of the long period of abstinence he'd gone through. Adelsa dropped her hand to Ki's crotch and began stroking him. Ki did not try to control his body's quick response. His hands moved to Adelsa's soft, warm breasts, and as he caressed them, he let himself swell and grow rigid.

Adelsa's busy hands had brought Ki to a full erection. She continued to squeeze and stroke him while Ki felt the tips of her breasts grow firm as he continued gently rubbing with his fingertips.

Adelsa suddenly released Ki and fell back on the bed. She spread her thighs as she invited, "Come into me, Ki. I'm ready for you, even if I can't show it the way you do."

Ki kneeled and Adelsa guided him. When he thrust, she brought her hips up to meet his lunge; then she locked her ankles behind his back and tensed the muscles of her legs to draw him into her. For a long moment she held Ki's hips locked by her thighs in such a tight embrace that he was unable to move. Then she freed him and spread her thighs wide.

103

Ki did not hurry his lunges, but kept them slowly rhythmic until Adelsa caught the tempo of his drives. Now she began to lift her hips when Ki began a downward stroke.

Ki settled down to a long, steady stroking and prolonged his slow thrusts until he felt Adelsa's body beginning to quiver. Then, at the end of a slow, deliberate penetration, he simply held himself buried in her. Adelsa tried to lift her hips, but Ki's weight pressing against her made any movement impossible.

Panting, her head thrown back, Adelsa squirmed for several minutes as she tried to lift her hips. Ki could feel the ripples of her body, but he held her pinned firmly, buried in her pulsing, wet warmth. When Adelsa's trembling faded and ended and she lay quiet except for her stertorous breathing, Ki still did not move, but waited for several more moments to pass before he started thrusting again.

Adelsa responded at once to Ki's steady thrusts. Only a few moments passed now before Ki felt himself building again, responding to the quickening of Adelsa's gusty breaths and her increasingly frantic gyrations. Then Adelsa began moaning, and her moans grew into a single long, ecstatic ululation that came from deep within her throat.

Ki drove harder and plunged deeper as he speeded up the rhythm of his drives. Adelsa's moves grew frantic, her body jerking in sharp, convulsive upthrusts that Ki knew signaled her final, fast-approaching climax. He let his control go and for a moment or two drove with frantic frenzy while cries of ecstasy burst from Adelsa's lips.

At last Ki jetted and shudders shook his body. He held himself pressed against Adelsa's still-quivering form until his climax rippled to an end. Then for several minutes both he and Adelsa lay limp and totally spent.

"I think I have never been with a man such as you before, Ki," Adelsa whispered after they'd rolled apart and were lying side by side. "I would like for you to stay, perhaps even to become one of our people."

"That's not possible, Adelsa," Ki replied. "I have to go

back to my own people, the ones I'm traveling with. But I won't leave until we're sure the Chiricahuas aren't coming here to attack your friends."

"If they'd been following us they would have been here before now," she said. "I think it is safe for us to sleep a while."

"I suppose that's the best thing we can do," Ki agreed. "I sleep lightly. I'll hear their hoofbeats long before they get here. Let's sleep now, and be ready to face tomorrow."

★

Chapter 10

Jessie and Bruce reined in when they reached the top of the winding zigzag trace they'd followed up from the riverbed. At the top of the rise, the narrow, crooked trail ended at the edge of a broad ledge that ran along the base of a high stone bluff. In the east the dawnlight glow of the rising sun was beginning to brighten the sky. It silhouetted the ragged horizon where the deep blue was steadily fading to a lighter hue.

Jessie and Bruce exchanged glances when they saw hoofprints along the ledge, but neither of them spoke. They dismounted and started walking slowly, leading their horses along the ledge, which extended from the base of the rising bluff and followed its irregular contours. As they moved, they studied the ledge's surface, but even the closest inspection of the hoofprints that pocked it gave them no clues.

Only a few of the hoofprints were clear-cut; most of them were badly blurred. The hoofprints were so numerous and overlapping that at a first glance Jessie found it almost impossible to distinguish between them.

"Can you make anything of these tracks?" she asked Bruce after they'd walked for a few minutes. Bruce had been keeping close to the rim of the ledge while Jessie followed the high wall on the opposite side. Before he could reply she went on, "All I can tell is that a lot of horses have passed this way lately, and in both directions. But there's no fresh sign of a wagon or cart or anything that runs on wheels."

"That's just about the same thing I'm finding out myself," Bruce replied. "And if I do say so, after all the stray horses I've had to track down since I begun breaking them, I'm a pretty fair hand at following their hoofprints. But maybe I've been seeing something you didn't notice yet. There's just not many prints of shod horses on this trail."

"I've noticed that myself," Jessie said. "And unshod horses means Indians."

"It sure does," Bruce agreed.

Frowning now, she went on, "But it seems to me that a shod horse like the one Ki was riding would leave at least a few prints."

"I'd say so, too," Bruce agreed. "And except for one thing, they'd ought to be easy to spot."

"What one thing are you talking about?"

"Why, when a man's on a horse he adds more'n a hundred pounds of weight to his mount, unless he's a dwarf," Bruce explained. Then he went on, "Now, the ground along here's pretty hard, and that'd make it easy for a horse that didn't have a rider not to leave as good a set of prints."

"But why would Ki not be—" Jessie stopped short. A worried frown formed on her face as she went on, "That would mean something's happened to him!"

"It might," Bruce nodded. "And from what I've gathered out of the little bits of saloon talk I've heard here and there, the Indian Bureau's put some of the meanest redskins on God's green earth onto a reservation that's bound to be someplace close to where we are right now."

"Do you know where it is?"

Bruce shook his head. "Not right down to dotting an i or crossing a t. The country hereabouts is way off of my regular range, Jessie. Mostly what I know about these parts is the places down on the prairie that I've had to chase into

108

looking for stray horses, but I've picked up some bits and pieces of saloon talk about what it's like in this part along in here."

Jessie had been thinking while listening to Bruce. Now she said, "We've found Ki's trail once, so let's try to pick it up again. The one thing we're pretty well sure of is that he must be somewhere close by."

"You're right about that," Bruce agreed. "He hasn't been gone long enough to get very far away."

"Then suppose we try to follow the trail those Indians left," she suggested. "It's the only clue we've got right now to where Ki might be, and we'd be fools not to follow it."

"I feel about the same way," Bruce told her. "And I'd say it's about the smartest thing we can do."

"We'll just move slowly and study the trail as we go," Jessie went on as they swung into their saddles. After she'd settled back and gotten both feet firmly in the stirrups, she added, "One of us ought to ride outside along the edge of the drop-off and go a little bit ahead of the other."

"I can see what you're getting at," Bruce said quickly. "I'll make that my place."

They started moving ahead, keeping their horses to a slow, steady walk. They'd ridden only a short distance when Bruce twisted in his saddle and raised his voice a bit to say, "We're coming to something up ahead, Jessie, and I figured I ought to let you know so you won't be surprised when you see it."

"What kind of something are you talking about?" Jessie asked.

"Why, it's not anything to bother about, just a little Paiute village, maybe a dozen or so houses, if you can call 'em that. You can't see them yet because of the way the trail curves, but it looks to me like they've got Paiute written all over them."

"I don't know much about the Paiutes." Jessie frowned. "We don't have any around the Circle Star. But as I recall, they're peaceful, not like the Apaches."

109

"That's right," Bruce agreed. "And what we're coming to's not such a much of a place, and I don't see but two or three of 'em stirring around outside."

"Do you think we ought to stop and ask if any of them has seen Ki?" she asked.

"Well, I reckon it's worth a try. The first shanty's just a little way ahead."

Jessie saw the first huts of the settlement within the next few minutes. A man stood beside one of the nearest. Bruce pulled up his horse, and Jessie halted at his side in time to hear his first question.

"Talk English?" he asked.

Though the man standing beside the hut had been watching Jessie and Bruce, he acted as though he had not heard Bruce's question. He looked from Bruce to Jessie and smiled, bobbing his head up and down.

"Talk *español*?" Bruce asked this time.

Again the Indian smiled and nodded, but still said nothing.

"I don't think he understands either English or Spanish," Jessie said and frowned. "I wish I knew Indian sign language, but it's something I've never had time to learn."

"Well, it looks like I've sorta drawn a dud here," Bruce told her.

"That's pretty obvious," Jessie agreed. "So we might as well move on."

"My guess is that stopping any of them would likely just be a waste of time," Bruce said. "I'd imagine that a few of them probably speak a little English, but I'd be at a total loss to pick out the right ones. Let's move on ahead for a spell, even if the outlook's not real promising."

They toed their horses into a walk. The sky was brightening rapidly now, and while covering the next half mile or so, Jessie and Bruce passed several more of the Paiute houses. At most of them there were women kindling fires, obviously getting ready to cook breakfast.

110

Even before the last of the little dwellings was behind them, the trail narrowed as the upward slope of the ground grew more pronounced. The rocks that protruded from the face of the steep cliff that rose on one side of the trail grew more numerous, and the cliff soon became a high, forbidding wall of solid stone.

"Well, at least one of those Paiutes ain't as lazy as folks say they are," Bruce remarked. He pointed ahead to the figure of a man walking along the base of the bluff. "At least one of 'em got up early and started someplace."

"He looks to be in a hurry, too," Jessie replied. Then she asked, "Do you think it'd be worth our time to stop and ask him what the country's like up ahead? If he can talk anything but his own language we might get some inkling of where Ki could—" She stopped short, leaned forward in her saddle to peer for a moment at the moving figure, then exclaimed, "We won't have to ask him, Bruce! I know the way that man's walking too well to be mistaken! That's Ki!"

Before Jessie had finished speaking, she was spurring her horse ahead. Bruce dug his heels into the flanks of his own mount and followed her. Hearing the hoofbeats, the walking man turned, and even at a distance, Bruce saw that Jessie had been right. She'd already reached Ki and reined in when Bruce pulled up and stopped beside them.

"So that's where I spent the night," Ki was telling Jessie. "As soon as I woke up, I started back here for my horse. If the Chiricahuas did chase after us, they didn't get as far as the Paiute village."

"Where is your horse, then?" Jessie frowned.

"I hope it's where we hid it yesterday," Ki replied. "Just ahead, in a gap in the wall of this big bluff. We didn't want to leave a trail all the way to where the Paiutes live. For all we knew the Chiricahuas were chasing us. They might even be out looking for us now."

"I still haven't caught up with everything that happened to you, Ki," Bruce said. "But if there's a bunch of Chiricahuas after you, we want to get away from here as fast as we can.

111

They're about the meanest redskins we could run into!"

"We've got a little time," Ki told him. "From the bits and pieces I've picked up about them, the Chiricahuas don't like to move too much at night. It's not likely they'd be starting out to look for me until the sun's up."

"That doesn't mean we can waste time," Jessie cautioned him. "You said you hid your horse somewhere just ahead, Ki. The quicker we get started back to our camp, the better off we'll be."

Ki pointed to a ragged black fissure in the canyon wall a few steps in front of them as he said, "It's in there. So is another horse that I took out of the Chiricahua's herd when Adelsa and I were getting away from them. I suppose we'd better take both of them."

"Why bother with an extra horse, Ki?" Jessie frowned.

"We won't bother," Ki said. "I'll leave the other one with the Indian girl who helped me get away. I don't even know that she needs a horse or wants one, but she can trade for it with her own people, or even just lead it down to the river and set it free."

When Ki squeezed into the rock fissure, he discovered that the job of getting the horses out of it was a much harder job than leading them into it had been. The animals balked and reared up on their hind legs as best they could in the limited space. At last Ki called on Bruce to help.

"Take one of the reins off your halter, Bruce!" he called. "Or both of them, if you need to. Wrap them around this horse's tail and get far enough back so it can't kick you, then start pulling while I push!"

With both Ki and Bruce forcing the horses backward in the dark, narrow split, and only after what seemed to have been a long stretch of strenuous efforts, they managed at last to back the animals out of the narrow fissure and onto the trail. Then, with Ki mounted and leading the spare horse, they started back toward the Paiute village.

Adelsa was nowhere to be seen when they reined in at her hut, and they stopped only long enough to tether the spare horse at the rear of the little dwelling. Then they got back on the trail to the mesa, and by the time the sun had reached its zenith, they had reached the spot where Jessie and Bruce had cached their spare provisions before beginning their search for Ki.

Though none of them made any remarks about a need to hurry, despite their hunger after an exceedingly busy morning, they put together only a spartan but passable noonday meal. After they'd eaten their fill of dry soda crackers and summer sausage, they sat in silence for a few moments around the small square piece of canvas tarpaulin that served both as a food package and tablecloth. It was Jessie who broke the silence that had held sway while they were eating.

"We still have half the day left," she remarked and turned to Bruce as she went on. "You know more about the way the land lays than either Ki or I do. If we start now, can we get to the rustlers' hideout before dark?"

"I won't say we can and I won't say we can't, Miss Jessie," he replied. "Because I never have put in the time it'd take to find it. I've only scouted around up here a little bit, and all I can be sure about is that we're somewheres close to the place we're looking for."

"I'd think there must be a trail of some sort leading to their hideout," Ki said. "Even on this hard-baked dirt."

"There might be one someplace, Ki, but I sure haven't come across it yet," Bruce told him. "I ain't just making talk when I tell you that this bunch of rustlers is about the cagiest I've ever run into or heard about. But the best I've been able to figure is that they're right careful not to leave a trail that'd be even a little bit easy to follow."

"I suppose they take a different route to their hideout every time they're chousing a bunch of stolen horses there," Jessie said, a thoughtful frown drawing her brows together.

"Something like that, Jessie." Bruce nodded.

"I've heard of cattle thieves driving a herd in little circles, and about them backtracking or going over the same trail more than once with a stolen herd," Jessie went on. "But I haven't had a great deal to do with horse thieves."

"And I haven't, either," Ki volunteered. "But back in the days when your father was just getting the Circle Star pulled into shape, before he started fencing the range, a bunch of rustlers drove off a herd of prize cattle that he'd bought for breeding stock. They tried the herd-circling trick, but Alex juggled a lot of figures around and came up with a way to beat them at their own game."

"I remember Alex telling me about that when I was a child," Jessie said and nodded. "But I was too young then to think about remembering the figures he used. I hope you remember them."

Ki shook his head as he said, "I'm afraid I don't. Alex explained it to me, but that was a long time ago and we've never had to use it since the Circle Star was all fenced and we've had enough men to ride the lines."

"We'll have to circle, then," she frowned. "And the best sign we can hope for is horse droppings."

"When I found out the outlaws had a hidey-hole someplace around here I begun looking for it," Bruce said. "That's when I come up here the first time. I tried looking for droppings then, and didn't find any. I've come back more'n a few times since then, and I've run across some little heaps now and again, places where I figured they'd stopped for the night. But this is a big mesa, and the droppings was always so far apart and scattered out that they didn't give me much to go by."

"I'm not sure that's a bad sign," Jessie said thoughtfully. "As I see it, they must have a place somewhere, maybe a little valley that's in a place hard to get to, maybe on top of one of these two mesas up ahead."

"Neither one of them is all that big," Ki put in. "Our first job's going to be to find the trail to the top."

"All we have to do is ride around the base until we find it," Jessie said. "A trail up to the top of a mesa like this is very hard to hide. Then we'll spread out and look until we

114

find their camp, or headquarters, or hideout, whichever you want to call it."

"I don't imagine they've tried to hide it," Ki said. "From the little bit we've already found out, I'd bet there aren't too many travelers on these trails around here."

"You're very likely right, Ki," Jessie agreed.

"Once we're on top of the mesa," he went on, "if we don't run across their place right away, I've got a feeling that if we ride in a line of loops we'll run into their place without really having to search too hard."

"Line of loops?" Bruce frowned. "Now, that's something I never heard of. Maybe you better explain it to me, Ki."

"Jessie can do a better job telling you about it than I can," Ki said. "As far as I know, it was her father who invented or originated it, whatever you want to call it." Turning to her, he went on, "You don't mind if I ask you to do it, do you?"

"Of course not," she answered. "I'm not sure that Alex invented the idea, but I've never run into it on any ranch except the Circle Star. But it's really very simple."

Leaning forward, Jessie brushed her hand across a bare spot in the loose, sandy soil. Extending her forefinger she traced a short line of a half-dozen interconnected circles. At the end of the half-dozen loops she carried the line a few inches farther before dipping it below the first circles, then traced an identical line parallel to the first and a few inches below it. She repeated the process again before looking up at Bruce.

"If you'll just imagine that there are a few more lines over these or under them," she said, "and that the circles are several hundred yards across, maybe more, you'll see that whoever's ridden a horse on this pattern will get a good close look at any hoofprints or footprints they're hunting for."

"Why, that's better than riding zigzags," Bruce said. "I can sure see where it'd come in handy for picking up a trail on flatland like those mesa tops."

"That's the reason it works." Jessie nodded. "There's no possible way to avoid seeing a line of tracks across it."

"Well, I've learned something new," Bruce went on. "All a man has to do is pick out a landmark or two and go round and round for a while. If there's a fairly straight trail crossing any of those circles, even a blind man couldn't miss it."

"That's what Alex thought, too, Bruce," Ki said. "Now that you know what we'll be doing, suppose we separate. One of the big reasons for riding a line of loops is that it lets two or three riders cover a lot of country very fast." He turned to Jessie and went on, "Where do we want to start, Jessie?"

Jessie glanced around, looking for a landmark, and discovered that finding one was not easy in such a place. The mesa top did not duplicate the broken country through which the river flowed. Here she saw raw and generally barren level ground, a rugged series of low-rising hills, almost parallel lines of miniature hillocks no higher than a man's waist. In some spots the land rippled like tall ocean waves, or like the surface of a freshly plowed field after a heavy rain had passed over and smoothed its dirt clods. Elsewhere there were flat areas where big patches of light green *alisal* stood shoulder-high.

Such other grass as there was grew in thick, closely-spaced clumps, with a few small piñon trees here and there. The trees did not grow tall in such a rainless land. The highest might hide the head of a man standing up, while the tops of the smaller trees would reach only to his waist or his shoulders. One feature stood out above all others. Just off-center near the middle of the mesa top a tall jagged boulder broke the otherwise featureless horizon.

Jessie's inspection had taken only a minute or two. She turned to her companions and said, "Let's start our loops here. Ki, you go on a slant to the left, while Bruce goes to the right. I'll ride between you, and that way we'll be sure that we can always see one another. There's bound to be something here that'll give us a clue to where those horse thieves are, and it's just up to us to find it."

116

★

Chapter 11

Disappointment shaded Bruce's voice as he said, "Maybe you and Ki won't agree with me Jessie, but I think we've done the best we could. We've tried for a good long spell, but I don't see that riding all those loops got us much of anyplace."

"I'm as disappointed as you are, Bruce," Jessie told him. "Our time wasn't wasted, though. Even if we didn't find anything except a few hoofprints, riding the loops showed us that the stolen horses certainly must've been on this mesa at one time, even if they're not here now." Turning to Ki, she asked, "Don't you agree?"

"Yes, Jessie, I've got to," Ki said and nodded. "We'd have found them if they were here now. There's not a chance in the world we could've missed running across them."

While Ki talked a frown had been forming on Jessie's face. Her voice was thoughtful and she spoke very slowly when she asked, "What about the other mesa, Ki? The one that rises higher, at the back of this one. Is it possible we've been looking in the wrong place?"

For a moment Ki did not reply. When he finally spoke, his voice was as thoughtful as hers had been. He said, "It was this one the hoofprints led to, Jessie. And I'm sure we'd still be following them if this ground wasn't so rocky and baked so hard."

"Besides that," Bruce put in, "as far as I've ever been able to find out, there's no way to get on the higher one. Why, the walls of that second mesa go right straight up, except for the places where there's a crack or a little shelf."

"All three of us can't have been fooled," Jessie insisted. "And we can't be wrong about the few prints we've run across. They must've been made by Bruce's horses and the outlaws."

"I'd say it's pretty obvious that the rustlers know all the tricks there are about hiding hoofprints," Ki said and frowned. "What it's likely they did was to haze the horses into little bunches and keep them in places where the ground's baked too hard to take a hoofprint."

"But surely we'd have seen more signs than we did!" Jessie protested. "No fresh droppings, no fresh hoofprints. Even if it's been almost a month since they were stolen, there ought to be some kind of signs that Bruce's horses were here, Ki. I don't think it's possible for them to've done what nobody's been able to do before—worked out some new way to hide hoofprints, one we haven't learned about yet."

"You're talking about the rustler's dream, now," Ki said and smiled. "That's a saloon tall tale for tenderfeet."

"They wouldn't need to do anything new, Jessie," Bruce said. "The old tricks still work. A few tow-sacks to wrap the horses' hooves in is all they'd need to do the job."

"Maybe I'm just being stubborn," Jessie said. "The trail where we picked up what few signs we saw didn't have any forks, and if they'd turned off I'm sure that it's impossible for all three of us to have missed noticing it. Don't you agree, Bruce?"

"Sure I do." Bruce nodded. "Trails don't just drop off into thin air. And we didn't see any prints of the horse herd leading back down from this mesa we're on. When you stand back and look at the lay of the land, the only answer I can see is that the thieves took my horses up to that other mesa."

"But how did they do it?" Ki asked.

For a moment they sat in puzzled silence. Then Bruce said, "Far as I know, there's no way they could've, Ki. Like I told you a while back, when I was getting my little spread set up I did lots of riding around learning every inch of the land hereabouts. I recall riding around the base of this double mesa, looking for a way to go up to the top of the high one yonder, but I never did find one."

"Not even from the top of this one?" Ki asked.

"Well, I've rode over all the top of this one here, just like I rode all around the base of it," Bruce replied. "And so have you and Jessie now. If there's anyplace a horse—or a man, either—has found a trail up to that other mesa, we'd all have to be blind to've missed it."

"Of course, I'm sure that the outlaws know how to hide a trail," Jessie said, "but I'm certain they never learned the trick of picking up their horses and carrying them. Even if they were able to do that, their boots would sink in—"

Bruce broke in suddenly. "Wait a minute, Jessie. What you just said reminded me of something."

"I can't think what it would be, but I hope it's something helpful," Jessie said. "Go ahead, Bruce."

Bruce's voice was slowly thoughtful as he went on, "What you said about the outlaws coming up with new tricks got me trying to recall things. It might not be such a much, but there's one thing I saw when I first started noseying around up here that didn't make much sense to me. I'd plumb forgotten about it till you made that remark."

"What was it you saw?" Ki asked when Bruce paused for breath.

"A big windlass that's been anchored on a rock outcrop a little ways back from the side of that other mesa, where it joins this one. I run across it the first time I was up here. I couldn't see much use for it, and there wasn't any signs it'd been touched for a good long spell. It was all dirty, and it had a pretty good layer of dry dust on top of the dirt."

"But a windlass is only good for lifting ore out of mines, or lifting heavy loads on or off a ship," Jessie said.

"I'd call a horse a pretty heavy load to lift up onto the top of that higher mesa," Ki said.

Neither Jessie nor Bruce spoke for a moment. Then Jessie said to Bruce, "Don't feel too put out that you didn't think about using a windlass to lift a horse. It didn't occur to Ki or me either."

"And I certainly didn't see the possibility right away, when you first mentioned it," Ki admitted.

"You know, it's funny that none of us tumbled to it right off," Bruce said musingly. "All I could figure when I stumbled onto that windlass drum was that a bunch of prospectors had come up here figuring they might find a gold mine, a deep one, where they'd need a windlass to lift out the ore. Then when they didn't find anything, they went somewheres else."

"And just walked away, leaving the windlass?" Jessie asked.

"Well, big as it is, and all spiked down to that rock I mentioned, I just got the idea they thought it was too much trouble getting it loose to take it with 'em," Bruce answered. "I recall wondering at the time how they got that big heavy thing up here."

"What made you think it belonged to prospectors looking for gold?" Jessie asked.

"Why, I just didn't see how it could be used anyplace but a gold mine, Jessie," Bruce replied. "I put in a little spell doing some gold prospecting and mining when I was young enough not to have any better sense. A windlass like the one I saw has just got two jobs to do. One's getting a bunch of miners down a shaft the easiest way, and the other one is getting the miners out, along with the ore they've dug."

"Were there any signs that somebody had started digging on this mesa we're on?" Ki asked.

"If there was, I didn't see any. All I ever did see was that big windlass."

"And you're absolutely sure that there aren't any signs somewhere else up here? Signs indicating that prospectors had been at work?" Jessie frowned.

Bruce shook his head. He said, "It's just like I told you, Jessie. But I haven't rode over this mesa real good since the first time I looked at it."

Jessie said thoughtfully, "You know how Alex was, Ki. He always said that anything out of the ordinary needed a second look, just to be sure you weren't missing something important."

"He said something else that I remember, too," Ki put in. "When you think you've come to the end of a trail, start looking for anything out of the ordinary before you give up."

"Well, we seem to be at the end of the trail," Jessie went on. "And I'd say a windlass in a place like this certainly isn't ordinary."

"It's anything but ordinary," Ki put in. "Miners and prospectors don't just walk away and leave a valuable piece of equipment, especially when they've struck a dry hole and are leaving for good."

"That's true," she agreed. Turning to Bruce, she went on, "I think we'd better go take a look at your windlass. If what we're beginning to think is right, it might just be the most valuable clue we've found since we started looking around."

"Well, it won't take us very long to get to where I saw it, Jessie," Bruce told her. "On top of this mesa, anyplace you want to go's not but a short ride."

Within a few moments all three were mounted, returning to the juncture of the high mesa with the one they'd been so diligently exploring. As Bruce had said, the ride was a short one. Less than a quarter of an hour after they'd started, they were approaching the point where the higher mesa rose fifty or sixty feet above the surface of its larger companion.

"There's the windlass," Bruce said, indicating the inverted vee of its massive timber frame and the oversized drum centered in it. "You can see I wasn't stretching the truth none when I told you how big it was."

"I'll have to agree, it's a right good size," Jessie told him.

"Four-by-eight timber legs and eight-by-eight crosspiece," Ki said and frowned. "And anchored the way it is on that rock outcrop, it's strong enough to pull an elephant."

"Or lift a horse," Jessie added.

She'd toed her mount closer to the windlass. Swinging out of her saddle, she began giving the apparatus a more detailed examination. She could see at a glance that the hoisting gear had been designed and built by men who knew what they were about.

Each joint had been reinforced with metal plates or straps of heavy iron. A long metal cylinder or drum spanned the five-foot gap between the supporting legs, its axles on each end fitted into thick metal hubs. Outside the framework, the hubs were fitted with cast-iron cranks. The drum itself was streaked with rust where the pressure of the cable had scraped the metal's surface as it turned.

"From the little bit I've learned by looking at some of our Starbuck coal and gold mining operations, that windlass was made and anchored the way it is to handle exceedingly heavy loads," Jessie said as she turned away from the apparatus. "I wouldn't be surprised if it could lift an elephant!"

"It certainly could," Ki agreed. "And I'm sure we're thinking the same thing, Jessie. If it can lift an elephant, it can lift a horse."

"You'd need a block and tackle and a whole lot of heavy rope to do that," Bruce put in.

"That occurred to me, too," Ki said. "I've seen a lot of heavy cargo boxes being lifted aboard a ship by a block-and-tackle rigging that's worked with a windlass like this one. And almost all the big ships use one in their sail-raising rigging."

Jessie had not stopped surveying the mesa's walls. Frowning now, she turned to Ki and said, "The face of that upper mesa on this side isn't as smooth or as straight up and down as it is on the other side, Ki. And there'd have to be somebody up on that ledge up above before any of the jobs we're talking about could be done." Turning to Ki, she asked, "Do you see any signs that somebody's been climbing that steep wall?"

"Not from here," he replied. "I got some fairly close looks at it while we were riding loops, and I didn't see a sign of a trail anywhere."

Jessie had been studying the huge almost cylindrical face of the second mesa while Ki talked. Now she said, "Do you think it could be climbed, Ki?"

Ki took a step backward and began scanning the mesa's face. After he'd studied it a moment, he said, "I can see enough handholds and footholds from where we're standing to get up to that first big ledge. It's only twenty or twenty-five feet high, not a big climbing job."

"Maybe it doesn't look like a big job to you," Bruce said. "But I'd hate to be the one that'd have to crawl along that wall. It looks as bare and smooth as a baby's bottom to me."

"Take a closer look, Bruce," Ki replied. "Do you remember some of our talks while you were the foreman at the Circle Star, and curious about me practicing *karateka*?"

"That's been a while back, Ki," Bruce replied. "Maybe you better dot your i's and cross your t's."

"Among other things, I recall telling you about Daruma, who was the first *karateka*. I learned that he worked out some of the *kempo* holds by climbing sheer rock walls to develop the strength in his hands while he was creating the art of winning combats without weapons. I haven't forgotten the training I had in my *do*, Bruce."

"I'm sure that Ki wouldn't think about offering to try unless he's sure of what he can do," Jessie said quickly. Then she turned to Ki and asked, "You're positive it's not too risky?"

"You know that I've climbed places just about as bad as this one, Jessie," Ki told her. He gestured toward the face of the mesa's rising wall as he went on. "That big crack in the wall there and the ledge above it is about all I need. I'll just brace myself with my arms and knees to climb up along the crack. When I get to the ledge, I'll follow it as far as it goes. It might even get me all the way to the top."

"Then if you can see a way to get up that sheer wall at the bottom, let's find out if there's anything on the mesa that'll give us a useful clue," she said.

"I think I can manage," Ki told her. "It's certainly worth a try."

Turning back to Bruce, Jessie went on, "Will you give Ki a hand in putting our lariats together? While you're getting ready, I'd like to go down the slope a little way and see if I can find a place where we might get a better look at that wall Ki's going to climb."

Ki had already started for the horses to get the lariats. Bruce followed him, and the two men knotted the lariats together in a figure-eight hitch.

"You really think you can get up that stretch to the ledge?" Bruce asked him. He dropped his voice, and its tone was worried as he went on, "It sure looks tricky to me."

"There shouldn't be a great deal of trouble," Ki replied. "And we'd never know what we might be missing if we don't look over this mesa very thoroughly."

"Well, I got to admit there's a lot to what you say, Ki. Now, just tell me what you want me to do. This job's a little different from lassoing a steer or a horse, and that's about the only way I know to handle a lariat."

"I'll carry the rope on my back while I'm climbing," Ki told him. "And I've found that going up a steep place like that is a lot easier than coming down. There's bound to be a place up on that first ledge where I can anchor the rope. I'll get it set and drop the end down here where you and Jessie can use it to pull yourselves up."

"Well, the way you put it, it sure sounds easy enough."

"If you're worrying about Jessie, there isn't any need to. She can climb a sheer wall that way. I've seen her do it, and it doesn't bother her a bit."

"You know, I've been away from the Circle Star such a long time, doing so many things I never did before, that I guess I've sort of forgot what a good team you and Miss Jessie make," Bruce said, grinning ruefully.

They'd finished knotting the three lariats into one long rope by this time. Ki dropped one end to the ground and began forming it into a single coil. He draped the coil across his shoulder, its loop slanting across his chest.

"I'm as ready as I'll ever be," he told Bruce. "And the wall up to that other mesa's not going to change, so let's get started."

Jessie turned away from her study of the mesa's sheer wall when she heard Ki and Bruce approaching. "I think you can find enough handgrips to climb that wall up to the other mesa, Ki," she said. "It just looks bare when you first start looking at it. But I've seen you go up worse places than this."

"Don't worry, Jessie. It's been a while since I've done much climbing, but once you've learned how, you don't forget," Ki assured her. "And when I get up there, I'm sure there'll be someplace that I can tie this rope so that you and Bruce can come up, if I find anything interesting."

They walked to the base of the sheer wall of the upper mesa. Ki leaned back to study it for a moment or two, then stepped up to the steep rise and began climbing.

For the first ten or fifteen feet the slanting surface of small gravelly stones slowed his pace as his sandaled feet skidded every three or four steps. He reached the sheer rise of the wall itself and tested it by leaning backward and delivering a few hard kicks, which started a small mixed stream of sand and gravel flowing. Moving around the mesa's base to a long, rising slit in a massive stretch of stone, he saw the crack in the face a few paces away.

Stepping up to it, Ki leaned backward until he could see that the crevice widened slowly to the point where it ended, only a short distance from the overhanging ledge at the top of the mesa. Ki wasted no more time, but began

125

ascending the steep face by bracing his feet at opposite edges of the crevice and shifting his weight from side to side as he pressed close to the sheer rise and levered himself upward.

At best, his progress for the first dozen or so feet above the ground was slow. In places where the surface of the rock was jagged or rough, he could slip his knees into the crevice and free his hands in order to raise them. Over such stretches his upward progress was measured in inches. He was forced to reach above his head and close his muscular hands on the rim of the crevasse, push both knees into the slit and spraddle his thighs for a precarious support while he raised his hands and found a hold by which he could lift his body a few inches.

Suddenly, to Ki's surprise, he reached a hand into the crevice and found a handhold that he could grip firmly. Lifting his other arm, Ki groped on the opposite side of the widening crack and found a similar handgrip. Holding himself firmly, Ki raised one foot and thrust it into the crevice. His foot slid in, and when Ki raised himself by pressing down on the foot in the crack, he lifted his free leg and found a second niche, to accommodate its foot.

Ki peered into the widening crevice. It was shrouded in shadows, but even in the limited light he could see similar handholds and footrests that spanned the gap all the way to the top of the crevice.

Turning his head and bending toward the ground, he called, "Jessie! I think I might've found something important! Unless I'm wrong, we'll be able to get to the top of this second mesa without too much trouble."

★

Chapter 12

"What on earth have you found?" Jessie called in response to Ki's announcement.

"Something we've never even thought about, Jessie. It's going to give us the help we need to get up to the top of the second mesa."

"What did you find?" she asked.

"Before we ever got here, somebody else had the same idea we did about using this crack to climb to the top of the second mesa," Ki replied. "And they made it easy to get up by putting steps in this high wall."

"You mean steps like a ladder?" she asked. As she spoke, Jessie was scanning the hard, raw stone-studded side of the mesa. She shook her head, but said nothing.

"Very much like one," Ki went on. "They're deep in this crack and it'd be almost impossible for you to see from where you are now."

Bruce had been walking along the line where the two mesas joined, searching the towering wall with his eyes. When he heard the exchange between Jessie and Ki, he hurried back to join. Now he bent his head back as far as possible to look up at Ki as he asked, "You're sure these steps or ladder or whatever it is you've found will go all the way to the top? Because from here, I can't see anything like what you're talking about."

"When I was standing where you are now, I couldn't see much of anything, either," Ki replied. "But they're here, all right."

"I guess the only way to find out is to climb them," Jessie said. "Be careful, Ki. Look out for traps."

"Don't worry," Ki assured her. "If my hunch is right, it's not going to take us very much time to find the answers to a lot of the questions that've been bothering us."

Ki returned his attention to making the ascent to the top of the mesa. After finding the first of the man-made steps, he was not particularly surprised to discover that the hidden rungs and handholds in the crevice were set at regular intervals all the way to the top. Their positions shifted from one side to the other, in only a few stretches of solid rock, where there were no fissures or breaks.

Ki's progress was swift and easy, though he took the precaution of testing each step before trusting his full weight to it. Less than a quarter hour passed after he'd started his climb from the lower mesa until Ki was pulling himself up to the topmost rung of the hidden ladder. Before taking that last step, he raised himself slowly until the crown of his head was almost level with the second mesa's surface.

Bracing his feet carefully to hold his position, Ki levered himself upward for the final few inches that would lift his eyes above the mesa's edge. He spread his elbows until his arms were flat against the cliff, holding himself half-suspended on the ladder's rung, ready to drop out of sight just by relaxing the muscles of his arms. It was a readiness of caution, one that he'd learned during the long years when he and Jessie were in almost constant conflict with the vicious European cartel whose hired killers had murdered Jessie's father.

At last Ki raised his head the final inch or two that allowed him to scan the section of the mesa's floor in front of him and begin peering across the gently upslanting land. Though while he climbed Ki had been speculating about what he might find, he was totally unprepared for what he saw now.

Even before he'd raised his head above eye-level Ki glimpsed the outline of a building. He muscled himself higher, his eyes moving from side to side, but there was no hint of motion anywhere he looked. Then he lifted a foot to the next rung and reared higher. Instantly, his field of vision expanded, for now his head was completely above the mesa's surface.

Ki spent a moment scanning the barren stretch beyond the building. It was a broken maze of yellowish sunbaked soil studded with boulders, small ones no bigger than a man's head as well as huge jagged hunks half-buried in the sterile soil. Beyond the stretch of featureless terrain there were a few gnarled trees and some stunted, pale green bushes. There were some patches of grass, but the shoots were short, evidence that horses or steers had been grazing on them.

Returning his attention to the building, Ki's quick inspection told him it was large and that the wall he faced was broken by several windows. He also noticed for the first time that a three-strand barbwire fence extended in both directions from the corners of the building's back wall. The barbwire strands formed a long, wide vee and stretched away from the walls as far as the uneven boulder-strewn ground of the mesa top allowed him to see. Ki guessed that the fence must span the mesa top from rim to rim.

Then Ki raised himself to the next upward step and directly ahead of him saw a tall tree trunk. All the branches had been sawed off and the long trunk slanted downward from its tip to its base. At the rear it was supported above the ground by a large iron bar that went through the trunk and rested on sturdy vertical posts on each side of its base. Against the base large boulders had been piled to give it additional strength and support.

A windlass, the mate of the one that Bruce had discovered on the lower mesa, rose near the base of the slanting tree. As Ki continued to shift his gaze from point to point around the astonishing contrivance he saw that there was a tangle of ropes and block sheaves at the tree's top.

Ki had traveled and worked on sailing ships in his own land. He'd also made enough voyages with both Jessie and her father to recognize the equipment. When in his mind he added the windlass to which Bruce had led them on the mesa's base to the gear he now saw on its top, he knew he'd confirmed the answer to the puzzles that had been perplexing both him and his companions.

What the horse thieves had done here, hundreds of miles from an ocean port, was to use the method evolved years ago to hoist horses and cattle from the shore onto a ship in ports where it was impossible simply to lead the animals aboard across a gangplank. The only difference was that the animals were lifted from the lower mesa to its much higher twin.

Twisting in his footholds, Ki leaned away from the mesa's rim as he called, "Jessie! You and Bruce are going to have to come up here! Tether your horses a pretty good distance away from these steps I'm on."

"What have you found, Ki?" Jessie called back.

Before Ki could answer, a drumming of hooves reached his ears. By the time he'd switched his hold to swivel his shoulders and gaze across the mesa, a small herd of riderless horses had appeared, galloping toward him. Ki's expert judgment, honed on the Circle Star, told him that there were at least twenty horses in the advancing herd.

Again Jessie's voice reached him above the thunking of hooves, which was growing louder now. "Ki!" she called, "am I losing my senses, or do I hear horses galloping up there?"

Ki had quickly overcome his wave of surprise. He swiveled to answer Jessie's question. "You're not hearing strange noises, Jessie. Yes, there's a herd of horses coming toward me right this minute."

"Well, I sure hope mine're in that herd!" Bruce called. "Even if I'm still not real sure I can believe what I'm hearing!"

"Your ears aren't deceiving you," Ki replied. "But don't you or Jessie bother starting to climb up here. As soon as I get on top of the mesa, I'll send the elevator down for you."

"Ki, this is no time to make jokes!" Jessie scolded.

"I'm not joking," he answered. "Just give me a few minutes to work, and I'll prove it to you."

"Why can't you tell us what you've found?" she asked. "It's not like you to evade something this way!"

Ki did not reply at once, for by this time the horse herd had reached the barbwire strands. They began scattering along the barrier as they whinnied and neighed for attention. As Ki climbed the last few feet of the ladder and stepped away from it to the top of the mesa, the animals began stirring restlessly and their whinnies increased. He made a quick tally and decided that there were at least twenty or twenty-five animals in the herd.

Ignoring the horses for the moment, Ki busied himself examining the clutter of gear that lay around the tree trunk. It had not been completely visible to him from the spot where he'd stopped, but now, guided by his memories of the sea voyages he'd made in the distant past, he began to bring order into the confused heap of lumplike blocks and sheaves and tangled ropes.

Within a surprisingly short time he'd straightened the two-inch rope, actually more cable than cordage, and the block sheaves that were attached to it on both sides. He continued his work, carefully untwisting the seemingly endless yards of ropes of various lengths and sizes.

The large two-inch ropes were stubborn and unyielding until the smaller inch-thick ropes had been straightened out. As Ki worked, the cordage that had been in such a baffling tangle became easier to work with. While his job progressed and he straightened out the ropes and the sheaves through which they ran, he worked out in his mind the functions that each set of them performed.

Far sooner than he'd thought possible, Ki found himself at the end of the job he'd assumed. He pulled the end of the rope wound on the windlass along the ground to straighten it, and at last the strange contrivance took on its final shape. He was holding hoisting gear designed to lift and lower heavy loads between the mesa he was now on and the one below it.

Only a few more minutes of work saw the heavy cable and the auxiliary ropes running smoothly through the sheaves. Then Ki took several turns of the key cable around his hips and moved to the windlass. He had little trouble finding the manner in which the rope should be laid on the ground before being used. Ki wasted no time. He fastened the end of the master rope to the eyebolt on the cylinder in which it so obviously belonged and stepped out of the coils he'd wound around his waist.

Now he moved to the windlass's crank and began turning it slowly. The slack straightened to the pull of the rope; then the double-geared blocks began to turn a few inches at a time. After a brief period of slow cranking, the rope grew taut as the full weight of the tree trunk began to make itself felt. For several minutes the hoisting gear seemed to fight Ki's best efforts, but at last a long thin triangle of daylight appeared between the tree trunk and the ground where it had been laying.

Setting his jaw doggedly, Ki began lifting himself off the ground with each rotation of the crank to add his weight to his strength. Slowly but steadily the treetop climbed to a higher point and began to show a sharper upward slant as the trunk rose slowly above the ground. Ki continued his stubborn efforts and the top of the big tree rose higher with each turn of the crank.

Then the blocks lifted the tree trunk to its balance point. After it reached and passed that critical area where the inside gearing of the block sheaves began turning readily, their double-geared mechanism multiplied Ki's own considerable strength, and the job became easier. At last the tree trunk reached an angle wide enough to encourage Ki to move to the next part of his job.

Securing the heavy cable in an eyebolt to anchor it, Ki stepped to the edge of the mesa to call Jessie and Bruce. When he peered over, he saw their upturned faces, but before he could say anything Jessie spoke.

"Ki, what on earth have you been doing up there all this time?" Jessie called when she saw his face peering down at her and Bruce.

"I've been working," Ki replied, his voice calmly level.

"Yes, we could hear you moving around, and we saw that big tree trunk moving, but couldn't imagine how you were doing it," Jessie went on. "And you still haven't told us—"

Ki broke in. He said, "You'll understand everything in just a few minutes, Jessie."

"I'm finding it awfully hard to believe what I'm seeing, too, Ki," Bruce put in. "What's that big tree trunk doing standing up on one end?"

Before Ki could reply, Jessie said, "Bruce and I decided it'd be foolish to interrupt you with a lot of questions, but we've both been burning up with curiosity!"

"I think I've found the answer to a lot of things that've been puzzling us, Jessie," Ki replied. "And to save a lot of explaining, I'm going to send the elevator down to bring you and Bruce up so you can see this place for yourselves."

"Elevator!" she exclaimed. "Ki, have you gone mad, or is this some sort of joke?"

"No, I'm serious," Ki called back. "Just stand away from the base of the mesa for a minute or so and I'll have you both up here quicker than you'll believe."

Stepping back from the mesa's rim, Ki went to the windlass and freed the crank from its retaining loop. The block sheaves grated and rasped as he gave the crank a half turn to lift the tree trunk high enough to be sure it would clear the mesa's surface. He locked the crank in its restraining leather loop while he turned the windlass's drum. Then he started cranking, and loops of rope began to encircle the drum until the tree trunk was hanging over the rim of the mesa. Then Ki paid out the rope hand over hand, letting the tree trunk's

133

own weight pull it slowly to the ground.

When the cable quivered and began to grow slack, Ki locked the big drum in place and stepped back to the edge of the mesa. Jessie and Bruce were standing beside the tree trunk now, gazing up along the taut line of the cable.

"Get on the tree trunk and hold on," Ki called. "The elevator's ready to bring you up."

"You're going to hoist both of us up at the same time?" Jessie asked.

"Of course. This gear was designed to lift a horse, and you and Bruce together don't add up to as much of a load as a horse would. Jessie, you stand on one end of the log; Bruce can get on the other end. You'll have to hold onto the cable for balance, and you'll have to remember not to move your feet, but I'll raise you very slowly."

When Jessie and Bruce were safely on the log, Ki began turning the windlass. Though he had to use more strength to hoist the heavier load, the faces of Jessie and Bruce became visible in a surprisingly short time as the crude elevator lifted them above the edge.

Ki turned the crank the last few revolutions needed to allow him to lock the windlass's cylinder and started toward the drop-off, his hand extended to Jessie. She grasped it and stepped off onto the mesa. Bruce followed her at once.

"How in the world did you get all this gear together and put it to work?" Jessie asked Ki as she surveyed their new surroundings. Then she shook her head and went on, "Never mind, Ki, explanations can wait." As Jessie spoke, she was surveying the section of the mesa beyond the hoisting gear. She saw the horses beyond the barbwire strands, and the building that stood at the top of the gentle upslope. With a gasp of surprise she exclaimed, "We've found the rustlers' hideout! And now that we're looking at it, I can see that it's no wonder they were able to make horses they stole disappear so mysteriously!"

"We've had a lot of questions answered." Ki nodded. "So many that I don't believe we have a lot more to ask."

Bruce as well as Jessie had been looking at their surroundings. Now he said, "I just can't believe this! But I can sure see now why I never could locate those damned scoundrels!"

"I have a hunch you'll find the horses that they stole from you are in the herd I saw a little while ago," Ki told him. "They've scattered now, but as small as this mesa is, we shouldn't have any trouble rounding them up."

"And I'd imagine we'll find some very interesting things in that building over there," Jessie went on. "I know you haven't had time to take a look at it, so why don't we just go and do that right now?"

"Suppose you and Ki go look at their place," Bruce suggested. "Me, I'm a lot more concerned about finding my horses."

"I can't blame you for that, Bruce," Jessie said. "Go look for them by all means. While you're doing that, Ki and I will go and see what we can find in their hideout."

They walked up the slope together and ducked between the barbwire strands. Bruce waved and walked on a slant away from his companions, heading for a little bunch of a half-dozen horses grazing a short distance away. Jessie and Ki moved slowly along the front of the building until they reached a door. It was fastened by a splinter of wood dropped through the eye of a ring bolt to secure the hasp.

"Obviously, nobody's at home," Ki said as he pulled out the splinter and swung the door open. "But just in case I'm wrong, Jessie, let me go in first."

Without waiting for Jessie to reply, Ki cracked the door open and stepped inside. A single quick glance around the big rectangular room he'd entered showed him that none of the rustler gang was inside. He moved aside and swung the door open a bit wider to let Jessie join him.

"Wouldn't you guess that the rustlers are out stealing more horses?" she asked Ki after she'd given the interior a sweeping look that took in its few features.

"Oh, I'd do more than guess, Jessie," he answered. "I'd say we can just take that for a fact."

There was very little for them to look at in the rustlers' headquarters. A wood-burning stove stood near the center of the back wall, where its heat would be most evenly distributed during the rare cold nights of the Nevada desert. A half-dozen narrow single beds stood head-to-foot along the same wall, three on either side of the stove. Hanging from nails driven into the wall above each bed was a miscellany of clothing: shirts, Levi's, a few denim jackets.

At each end of the room other nails had been placed in the walls, their spacing indicating that they supported rifles when the rustlers were in residence. The windows in the wall where the beds were aligned were grimy; here and there the glass had been cleaned in small areas, obviously to allow those inside to look out when moisture fogged the panes.

"Let's see what we can turn up in here that might help us find out a bit more about our enemies," Jessie suggested. "I don't have much hope of running into anything, though I'd say that whoever's leading this outfit must be a bit smarter than the ordinary run-of-the-mill horse thief."

"Yes, if it was the leader who had the idea of hiding stolen horses here," Ki agreed. "He's not only smart enough to've found this place, but it was very clever indeed for him to think of using that old ore hoist to lift them up here."

"Even if I don't like to give horse thieves any kind of compliment, I've got to admit you're right, Ki," Jessie said. "They were smart enough to recognize a place where the horses didn't need men to herd them, couldn't stray, and where nobody would be likely even to dream of looking for them. But we're wasting time standing here talking. Why don't we look around and see what we can find?"

★

Chapter 13

"This place is pretty bare, Jessie," Ki said, gesturing to their surroundings with a sweep of his arm. "So it shouldn't take us long to go over it thoroughly. Where do you want to start looking?"

"I can't see that it makes much difference," Jessie replied after she'd glanced around the long rectangular interior of the hideout. "There aren't any closets to dig into, and a kitchen table along with a few straight chairs don't provide many hiding places."

"All we'll need to look into are the cookstove, the beds, and the clothes hanging along the wall," Ki said after a second quick look around the room. "It certainly shouldn't take us very long to go over all of it pretty thoroughly."

"If there's anyplace where you could hide something bigger than a pocket handkerchief, I can't see it," Jessie went on. "That stove is about in the middle of the back wall, Ki. Why don't we make it our dividing line? You take the side of the room that has the door in it, I'll go over the other half."

Wordlessly, with the easy silence of teamwork long proved in hunts far more dangerous and challenging than the one in which they were now engaged, Jessie and Ki began their search.

Jessie was standing closer than Ki to the stove. She stepped up to it and opened the oven door. A rancid odor swept out and she turned her head aside for a moment. When she looked back at the oven after she'd overcome the first nausea brought on by the stench, she located its source at once. It came from a thick layer of rancid grease shining from the bottom of the oven.

One quick glance showed Jessie that the baking chamber was empty except for three or four tin pie plates on the racks and a grimy pot with its bottom buried in the layer of grease. She stepped away from the stove quickly and waited for the odor to dissipate. It seemed to follow her and hang in the air even when she took another backward step to put a bit more distance between her and the cookstove.

"I can tell you two things these outlaws don't have, Ki," she called across the room. "One is a dishpan and the other is somebody who doesn't mind using it."

"Yes, I can smell that from here," Ki said. "But in this hot country rancid grease is pretty much a part of any kitchen stove you might run into."

When the odor finally dissipated, Jessie returned to the stove and finished examining it. When she'd completed her scrutiny, she'd learned just one thing: except for the utensils in the oven and on top of the stove, there was nothing to inspect. Stepping away from the stove, she stopped at the bed nearest it.

A pair of faded Levi's and a butternut-brown shirt hung from a nail above the tousled blankets. Leaning to reach the wall, she ran her hand experimentally along the garments. Her fingers encountered a round object in one of the pockets of the trousers, easily recognizable as a coin.

She ran her hand into the pocket and drew out her find, looked at it and discovered that it was not a coin, but a milled round of copper. On one side the figure "1" stood out in low relief, on the other there was the inscription *MABLE'S— SEARCHLIGHT, NT.*

138

"Ki, I know there's a big gold mine at a town called Searchlight, and that it's not terribly far from here," Jessie said. "But I don't remember exactly where it is. Do you?"

Ki did not reply immediately. Then he said, "It's down in this little corner of the Territory, not too far from where we are now, maybe a very long day's ride on a good horse. The mine's a very old one; it's been worked for a long time. Why're you asking? Have you found something that would give us a reason to be interested?"

"There's a whorehouse token from Searchlight in a pocket of these trousers I've been searching," Jessie answered. "I don't know how far these men go to steal horses, but it's pretty certain that the fellow who sleeps in this bed has been to Searchlight fairly recently. At least, I suppose this token's recent. There isn't any sign of wear on it and the brass has that shiny new look. It'd be a long shot at best, but maybe it's a clue to where we could look for the outlaws if they don't come back soon."

"We certainly won't have any trouble finding Searchlight," Ki told Jessie. "It's only a long day's ride from here, to the northwest. I was there a long time ago with your father, when he was just beginning to expand his mining interests. He wanted to look at the place because he had an idea that he might want to make an offer to the Sunshine Mine. The owners weren't interested in selling, so Alex didn't press them. He just bought mines in other places."

"We might keep Searchlight in mind, though, if we don't have any luck here finding where the rustlers hid their money. If there's a bank in Searchlight, that might be where they put their loot before dividing it up." Jessie was silent for a moment or two; then she went on. "But we can always talk about that later. Let's hurry and finish searching this place, Ki. When we're through we'll look for Bruce and see if he's had any luck finding his horses."

For the next half hour Jessie and Ki worked in their usual companionable silence. Now and then one of them commented on some unusual object found in the pocket of a shirt or a pair of jeans, or a stash box under one of the beds: a Jew's harp, a silver dollar that bore the cup-shaped mark where it had been hit with a rifle or pistol bullet, a lock of hair, an old daguerreotype so purpled with age that the image it had borne was indistinguishable. When the last bed and the final garment had been inspected, Ki turned to Jessie.

"I don't see that we know much more about those outlaws than we did when Bruce came to the Circle Star looking for help," he said. "And there's not any sign of a place where they've hidden their loot. What's our next move, Jessie? Shouldn't we start trying to find Bruce?"

"He's certainly had time to look for his horses," Jessie said. "But even if he's found all of them, it's going to take quite a while to get them down to the lower mesa. That windlass can only handle one animal at a time."

"Yes, that's a job we'd better start as soon as we can," Ki agreed.

"Suppose we give this place a final quick look, then," Jessie suggested. "I'm sure there's something we've been overlooking, but short of tearing up the floor, or—" She stopped short, a thoughtful frown forming on her face.

Ki's frown was as puzzled as Jessie's while he watched with a silence that matched hers. At last she went on, "The floor, Ki. We've pulled all the bedding off the beds to see if there was anything in the mattresses. We've looked at the table and the stove and all the chairs. But if you didn't have a safe and were hiding money, most of it in heavy gold or silver coins—"

"You'd put it under the floor, of course!" he broke in. "And that's one place we certainly haven't given too much attention."

No more words were needed. Both Jessie and Ki dropped to their knees. Moving slowly on all fours, they started inspecting the wide floorboards, inch by inch. Ki crawled in one direction, Jessie in the other, both of them describing zigzags from the end walls to the center of the long narrow room. They looked under each bed as well as inspecting the area along the walls between the beds.

Each of them had covered a good expanse of the bare boards and floor and were beginning to search under the beds when Jessie called to Ki.

"I think I've found what we've been looking for," she said. "It may not look like much, but it's the only mark I've run across that I can't understand. Come and take a look."

Ki stood up and stepped to Jessie's side. She was still kneeling beside the bed that took up most of the end wall. As Ki dropped to his knees beside her, Jessie pointed under the bed to indicate a joint where two of the wide floorboards were butted together.

By twisting around and bending closer, Ki could now see the heads of the nails in the boards, and he saw as well a few small dents in the planks and two or three long, shallow grooves where the butted ends had been splintered. He recognized them just as Jessie had, as places where the end of the marred board had been pried into, probably with a knife blade, to lift it.

"I think you've found the horse thieves' stash, Jessie," Ki said.

While he was speaking, Ki was slipping a *shuriken* from the leather case strapped to his left forearm. Jessie bent closer to watch as he inserted the edge of the blade into the almost invisible crack where the butted boards came together. Ki pressed the top arc of the *shuriken* gently; then, as the wide plank tilted a fraction of an inch, he gripped the narrow edge of the board with his fingertips and pulled it slowly upward.

To Ki's surprise the board lifted easily. When he saw that he could slide the fingers of his free hand into the crack he'd created beneath the board, Ki supported it long enough to lay the *shuriken* aside and used both hands to lift the board free. Even in the faint light that removing the board had allowed to trickle into the cavity that was now exposed, both Jessie

141

and Ki could see the gleaming yellow of gold and the bright sheen of silver coins.

"This is where they've been hiding their money, all right," she said. "And from what we're looking at here, they have most of it in gold. I can see a few cartwheels and some half dollars, but not many."

"Yes, I noticed that, too," Ki agreed.

As he spoke, he was pushing his hand into the space between the floorboards and the gold stash. There was barely room for Ki to slip his arm into the gap between the floorboards and the gold. As far as he could reach, Ki felt nothing except round cold coins. He persisted in his efforts for a moment, then withdrew his arm and sat up on the floor. Looking at Jessie, he shook his head.

"You can't feel the sides of the box?" Jessie frowned.

"Not in any direction I've tried, Jessie. As far as we know, the entire space under these floorboards is covered with gold and silver coins, and I have a hunch that we can only reach a very small part of it."

"Whoever planned this hiding place was very clever, Ki," Jessie said. "He's made sure that anybody who wants all this thieves' loot will have to spend a lot of time tearing the place up. I'm like you; I don't have any respect for horse thieves, but we'll have to admit that these outlaws—or maybe just their leader—was very shrewd in working out this way to protect their loot."

"What do you think we should do, then?"

"We didn't come up here looking for outlaws' gold, Ki," Jessie replied after a moment's thought. "We came to get Bruce's horses back from the bunch that stole them. I'd say let's just leave the money alone for the time being and go find Bruce. We'll help him round up his horses, then lower them down to the other mesa. While we're doing that, we can be thinking about all this money."

"You're right," Ki agreed. "We'll get the horses off our minds first. After they're safely down to the lower mesa, we can decide what we want to do about this outlaws' nest."

142

While he and Jessie talked, Ki had been restoring the floor to its original condition. When he'd satisfied himself that his work would pass inspection, he stood up and said, "I think we've done all we can here, Jessie. Let's go see if we can find Bruce."

Stepping outside the door, they stood looking from one side to the other of the gently slanting mesa top.

"Bruce went off that way," Jessie said, indicating the eastern side of the mesa. "He was so anxious to find out if those horses the outlaws stole from him were really up here that he couldn't wait to get moving. Why don't we just go in the same direction?"

"It's as good a way as any," Ki agreed. "The mesa top's not all that big. It shouldn't take us long to cover it."

Jessie and Ki began walking over the hard ground. Despite its packed surface, the dense yellow soil held enough shallow hoofprints to confuse them as they tried to find the boot prints Bruce must have left when he began his search for the horses.

Now and then they spotted a few of the tight arcs pressed into the soil that had been left by Bruce's boot heels; there were enough of these to keep them going in what they were reasonably sure was the right direction. Then after a long period of aimless zigzagging, as Jessie and Ki tried to pick up the boot prints when they'd faded on an unusually broad rock outcrop, the prints vanished entirely.

"We'll have to circle away from the fence here," Jessie said. She gestured toward the downslope beyond the fence. "I'd guess that the top slants down from here to the point where we came up, Ki."

"It certainly looks that way," Ki agreed. "Let's angle toward the other edge of the mesa. In the space we're limited to, we can't very well miss seeing Bruce."

They turned away from the fence. The search that they were starting now was like others they'd made in the past, though it was infinitely easier than some. They did not need to discuss what they would do. Ki moved away from Jessie just as she turned in the opposite direction. They walked slowly, zigagging at angles that would allow them to cover different areas of the mesa top while still keeping within sight of each other. Although they were mounting an upslope now, both of them walked faster than they had before.

Though for the most part the terrain underfoot was expanses of solid rock broken by patches of gravel, there were a few places where earth covered the stony sections, and now and then they passed small patches of pale green, more a fuzz of grass than a growth, on what at first glance appeared to be barren strips of small gravel separating islands of solid rock.

"You know, Ki, there must be water under the surface of this mesa," Jessie remarked on one of the occasions when their zigzagging paths brought them close enough to one another to allow them to talk without shouting.

"Yes, in this country water's where you find it, not in streams, but in little pools," Ki agreed. "And as a lot of miners have learned, there's a surprising amount running through rock fissures underground."

"I suppose—" Jessie broke off as a horse's whinney somewhere ahead of them broke the silence. Then the upraised voice of a man reached their ears from somewhere beyond the jagged outline of a ledge they were approaching. Jessie went on, "I think we've finally found Bruce, and from those whinneys, I have an idea he's come across some horses."

"It certainly sounds that way," Ki agreed.

Jessie was moving faster now. Ki increased his own pace. They were approaching the beginning of a long, low upslope, and as they moved toward its crest, the whinneys sounded louder. Taking long, quick steps now, they hurried up the rise. Even before they reached its crest, they could see the backs of several horses, and now and then one would rear upward to give them a glimpse of its ears, or its rump.

Then they reached the top of the slope and looked down. On a wide shelf below there were perhaps a dozen horses milling around, and at the center of their sleek backs and rumps and riffling manes, they got their first glimpse of Bruce. He was chasing the horse nearest him.

For a moment, Jessie and Ki froze in astonishment at the sight below them. Above the top of his boots, Bruce's legs were bare almost to his crotch. He was moving in whirls and zigzags as he tried to get a firm handhold on the mane of one of the milling horses. At last he succeeded, and both Jessie and Ki hurried to help him.

Ki reached the horse before Jessie did. He grabbed the animal's mane at the base of its neck. Ki and Bruce had firm holds now, and with its head held firmly, the horse suddenly lost its urge to buck and swivel. Jessie had stopped a short distance away, and as soon the animal grew calm, she came up to its head and looked questioningly at Bruce.

"What can I do to help?" she asked.

"Why, if you'll just spell me for a minute and hang on to this stubborn cuss, I'll get a noseband on him, or what passes for one," Bruce replied.

With Jessie and Ki to keep the animal's head steady, Bruce had little trouble looping and knotting the makeshift halter in place. Though now and again the horse tried vainly to toss its head in protest against the feel of çloth instead of the usual metal bit between its jaws, it did not buck or resist, but stood quietly while Bruce completed his job. He stepped back and gestured for Jessie and Ki to release their holds.

"Are you sure it's safe to let go?" Ki asked.

"Safe as it'll ever be," Bruce answered. "Them other ones I got rigged out don't seem to mind, but they've had time to get used to the different feel."

"I can see now why you're wearing such short trousers." Jessie smiled. "But it looks to me that ripping off the legs of your jeans has given you a pretty good start at getting back your stolen horses."

"Well, I was a fool not to think about carrying along a coil of rope when I set out, and I had to keep my lasso on hand because I needed it to get the horses with. But about all I had on my mind was getting these broncos in some

145

sorta shape so's I could lead 'em," Bruce told her. "So I just cut the legs off of these Levi's with my Barlow knife and sliced 'em up to make me some tethers."

"A pair of Levi's isn't what I'd call a big price to pay for getting your horses back," Jessie agreed. "But I hope you've got a spare pair in your saddlebags or your legs will be blistered a long time before we get back to your home place."

"I got spares, Miss Jessie," Bruce assured her. "And if you or Ki don't mind giving me the lend of a real lariat, I'll get the rest of my horses ready to go real quick."

"Why, of course!" Jessie said. "How many more do you have to catch?"

"Just four out of this bunch," Bruce told her. "At least that's all I got a look at. There was more on my spread that I'd got to the point where I could sell 'em, but I ain't caught sight of them anyplace. Dear God only knows where they might've got off to up here."

"Then suppose you use Ki's lariat and I'll use mine to help you catch them," Jessie suggested. "We certainly don't want you to go back and leave a half-dozen good horses here on this mesa, but we don't have any idea when those outlaws will be coming back. If it's possible, we don't want to get into a showdown shootout with them."

While Jessie and Bruce talked, Ki had been looking over the horses that were bunched around them. Now he turned to Jessie and said, "You take my lariat and Bruce can use his. I'll swing around and take a look. Maybe I can find the rest of the horses. They're all branded, aren't they, Bruce?"

"Oh, sure," Bruce answered. "There won't be a bit of trouble telling my horses from what few're up here right now."

"Remember those spare lariats we saw back at the outlaws' place, Ki?" Jessie asked. "You can use them to tether the horses Bruce has already caught. Then as soon as you get them safely put away, you can come back. With both of us helping Bruce look for the rest, it ought not take too long for us to round them up."

146

★
Chapter 14

Somehow Ki managed to get safely back to the outlaws' hideout without losing any of the horses that Bruce had captured. To his surprise the hastily improvised lead lines proved to be reliable instead of troublesome, even while he led the horses across the hard-baked, boulder-strewn ground that stretched in front of the outlaws' hideout.

When crossing that difficult section of ground, Ki had a few rough moments. The worst time he faced was a tense quarter hour when one of the feistiest of the broncos showed that it had its own ideas about going along with the others. The animal balked suddenly, and when it stopped moving, it began tossing its head aimlessly until its sudden moves snapped its makeshift tether.

Ki had handled enough balky half-broken mustangs on the Circle Star to know that he must respond quickly. He dropped his reins at once and dodged among the boulders until he could grab the recalcitrant bronco's ears. The horse whinnied protestingly as Ki led it to the others and retied the improvised lead rope. When he got the horses moving once more, the feisty pony followed without further trouble.

Its rebellion seemed to have inspired the entire herd,

though. From that moment on, one or another of the recaptured horses seemed determined to break away from the little herd each time the small cavalcade passed an unusually tempting patch of green grass. Knowing how fragile the lead lines were, Ki became wary of trying to force the recaptured horses. When one or another of them showed signs of restlessness, he waited until the uneasy mustang calmed; then he moved slowly on.

With the outlaws' headquarters in sight at last, Ki did not try to suppress a sigh of relief while he bunched the horses beside the building. He risked letting the recaptured animals stand while he went inside and took down the lariats that he and Jessie had seen when they were in the hideout earlier. Cutting them into short lengths, he improvised a passable headstall for the feistiest of his charges. When his first makeshift head harness proved to be successful, Ki used it as a pattern.

With fingers moving in quick flicks, he fashioned the gear needed to secure the remaining animals in a manner to which they'd now become accustomed. As soon as a harness was completed, Ki fitted it to one of the horses before leading the animal across the rock-strewn ground, away from the outlaws' hideout, to the small cleared area beyond the hoisting boom, and securing its makeshift harness to a low hitch rail that the horse thieves had placed there for their mounts.

His chore completed, Ki swung onto the back of one of the calmer horses. He was beginning to rein around and start to rejoin Jessie and Bruce when he glimpsed a flicker of movement near the bottom of the almost vertical decline that fell away to the surface of the lower mesa.

Now Ki moved by instinct long honed to be aware of unexpected threats. He let the reins drop before his horse could move away from the shield provided by the building. Sliding off its back, he waited only long enough to be sure the animal would stand in spite of its hurriedly formed makeshift harness; then he moved on foot to the end of the protecting bunkhouse. There he dropped belly-flat and began pulling himself forward by his elbows around the corner of the outlaws' hideout.

Keeping his head as low as possible while still allowing him to look down the precipitate drop, Ki began scanning the surface of the lower mesa. Looking from this height, he had no trouble spotting the outlaws and watching them. There were six of them, standing in a tight group close to their tethered horses a short distance from the point where the steep rise to the upper mesa top began.

Ki could hear their voices only in a muffled undertone, though now and then a stray word arose above their low-voiced discussion. After he'd watched for a few moments, Ki did not need to hear everything they were saying to follow the trend of their conversation. The bits and pieces that he did hear, coupled with his interpretation of an occasional gesture from one or another toward the windlass and then in the direction of the high mesa's top gave him the only clues required.

Only one interpretation of the outlaws' plans was possible: the horse thieves were getting ready to storm the top of the mesa, and this was no surprise. From the first moment that he and Jessie and Bruce had made their approach to the base of the upper mesa, they'd all been aware that they were leaving a trail that no one but a blind man could have missed.

Ki summoned up all his patience while he continued to watch the outlaw band. He knew that he was facing a choice of waiting and trying to stop the horse thieves in their approach, or riding back to alert Jessie and Bruce, who would even the odds by joining him in repelling the imminent attack.

Suddenly, Ki saw his options vanish as the horse thieves began to shift and move apart. One of them handed his rifle to a companion and started climbing the tricky foot trail that would bring him to the top of the upper mesa. It was no real job for Ki to deduce that the rustler had been delegated to operate the windlass while his companions covered him with rifle fire. Ki took the only choice that remained open to him.

Squirming around, he returned as quickly as possible to where he left his rifle. Pulling his rifle from its scabbard, he crab-crawled back to the mesa's edge. Though Ki knew that his progress would be slowed by his precautions, he chose to squirm along the ground in his effort to return to the mesa's rim before the outlaws had a chance to glimpse him.

By the time Ki reached his objective, he could hear the boots of an ascending outlaw scraping on the steep incline. He stopped and gauged the distance the outlaw still had to go; then he put aside his rifle, being sure it was within easy reach of his hand. He slid a *shuriken* out of its case and waited.

Gradually the crunching sounds of the approaching outlaw's boot soles on the slope grew louder. Ki could not locate them accurately by the sounds they made, and at that point he did not want to risk being discovered too soon. He began turning his head slowly from side to side to be sure he'd be looking at a point close to the spot where the climbing horse thief would first be visible. He was shifting his eyes from one side of the ridge to another when from the corner of his eye he saw the creased crown of the man's hat rising above the ground.

Ki shifted slightly to give himself a more direct throwing line to his approaching target. Now the outlaw's face was visible, less than a dozen long paces from where Ki lay concealed. Ki saw that the moment he'd been waiting for had arrived. He gripped his *shuriken* and rose to his knees, the hand holding the throwing-blade poised and ready.

When the outlaw saw Ki rising, he clung to his position with his left hand while his gunhand dropped to the butt of his revolver. Before he'd managed to bring the weapon high enough for a shot, Ki loosed the *shuriken*. The glistening tips of its razor-sharp points arcing through the air drew the horse thief's eyes away from Ki for a moment, and those few seconds when the outlaw turned his head were fatal for him. Ki's *shuriken* sliced through the renegade's hat and the thin skull bones above his ear, into his brain.

For a moment the climbing outlaw hung poised on the rim of the mesa. While the impact of a rifle slug would have thrown him backward, the more subtle severing of blood vessels and brain tissue by the slicing of the throwing-blade did not show its effects for several heartbeats. Then the dying rustler's gunhand sagged and the Colt plummeted down from it as his already lifeless body began tumbling in a final fall.

One of the rustler's companions must have been watching from the lower mesa, for as the man on the rim began toppling, a rifle shot cracked below. Its slug whistled past Ki's head, and he dropped flat in the fraction of an instant that passed before a second shot rang out from below. This bullet raised dust only inches from Ki's position.

Ki's ground-hugging posture gave him the shield of a few inches of the mesa's rim just as another shot rang out from below. Ki was no longer vulnerable, lying prone as he was on the edge of the drop-off. The bullet had no effect except to raise a puff of sandy dust below the edge of the rise a foot or so distant from where he lay.

Before the echoes of the shot had died away, hoofbeats thunking on the hard earth behind him drew Ki's attention. Knowing that they heralded the return of Jessie and Bruce, Ki twisted around, his cheek brushing the ground. He called, "Jessie! Bruce! I guess you know by now that the outlaws are bunched on the lower mesa! Don't get close enough to the rim for them to see you! Drop down and belly-crawl so they won't be able to get you in their sights!"

Jessie and Bruce dropped to their bellies. They were starting to crawl toward Ki when another rifle barked from below and its bullet raised dust less than a yard from the rim where Ki had stationed himself.

"Wasn't that a little bit too close to you for comfort, Ki?" Jessie asked as she and Bruce came to a halt beside him.

"It was pretty close, all right," Ki agreed. "But one or two others have been closer."

"We'd better be a little bit more careful, then," she suggested.

Jessie had hardly finished speaking before a second rifle cracked from below and the slug whistled above her head. She ducked involuntarily before realizing that it was a wild shot, fired on the off-chance that it might find a target.

Ignoring the near miss, she went on, her voice as calm as though she were asking the time of day, "We'd better be even more careful about staying back from that rim."

"It don't look to me like we can have it both ways, Jessie," Bruce said. "If they can't see us and we can't see them, we'll just be wasting shells."

"Which is something we can't afford to do," she agreed. "Those horse thieves have more guns than we do, and likely a lot more ammunition."

"Then we better be real careful about swapping shots with them fellows," Bruce suggested. "Because when we run out of what shells we got left there's not a way in the world we can get any more."

"Oh, I'll have to agree with you," Jessie confessed. "The horse thieves can't get up on this mesa to attack us unless they feel like making themselves sitting-duck targets, and we can't attack them without exposing ourselves."

"Which is another good reason why we can't afford to let this fracas just drag on and on," Bruce frowned.

"Of course not," Ki agreed. "But there's one good thing about it. Right now, we've got the high ground, even if it does keep us pretty well tied down."

"It's not the first time we've been caught in this sort of a standoff, Ki," Jessie reminded him. "And if we can't afford to risk making a move, neither can they."

"At least not until dark," Ki reminded them. "But there's still a lot of daylight left, and we'd better figure out a way to make the best use of it."

"I hope you've got some ideas," Jessie told him. "Because right now I can't seem to come up with one."

"All I can think about right now is gravity," Ki said and frowned. "We might not have much ammunition left, but we've certainly got plenty of rocks handy back there in front of their shanty."

"Ki, I know you well enough to understand that you're not joking, but throwing rocks at men armed with—"

"Give me just a minute more," Ki broke in. "It's not going to be too big a job or take a lot of time to roll the biggest of those rocks up here to the edge. All we have to do then is to start them down this steep slope and bombard those horse thieves with them. We just might be able to scatter those men, perhaps even drive them away, without firing a shot ourselves."

"You make it sound awfully easy," Jessie replied. Then she nodded thoughtfully and went on, "But there's not much doubt about you being right."

"Then suppose you keep an eye on the bunch down on the lower mesa while Bruce and I get some of nature's own cannonballs ready," Ki suggested. "It won't take us long to get them started down that steep drop."

"Let's do it the easiest way possible," Jessie suggested. "Why don't you and Bruce get up there and pick out the roundest ones, and start bringing them over there to the other end of the outlaws' shack?"

"You've got some ideas, Jessie?" Ki asked.

"One, at least," she replied. "If I'm not mistaken about the way the land lays, that's where the steepest slope is above the place where the outlaws are now. Since you started us thinking about a rock bombardment, I've gotten an idea that we might be able to get those rocks started rolling down the slope in two or three different directions."

153

"Bracketing our shots like field artillery," Ki said, his usually impassive face breaking into a smile.

"Exactly!" Jessie exclaimed. "We've decided what to do, so let's get busy doing it!"

"Remember to keep them guessing with a shot or two," Ki told her as he and Bruce turned away. "We'll have our own silent artillery ready for a barrage in just a few minutes."

Jessie nodded before turning and starting toward the position she'd chosen for what they hoped would be their surprise attack. When she reached the corner of the outlaws' hideout, she dropped to her hands and knees and began crawling toward the edge of the mesa.

A few moments brought her to within a half-dozen yards of the drop-off. She flattened herself on the ground and pushed herself forward with her booted feet before proceeding. When from her low-profile position Jessie could see the beginning of the shelf where the windlass was located, she stopped for a moment and studied the location of the biggest boulders at the edge of the mesa before proceeding, then continued inching forward until, by raising her head and shoulders a few inches, she could see the outlaws on the lower mesa.

Jessie divided her attention for another minute between the group of outlaws and the ground that fell away so sharply to the ledge below. She was still watching when Bruce reached her. He was pushing an ovoid boulder much bigger than his head, and now he shoved it within easy reach of Jessie's outstretched hands. Moving the big chunk of rock with more than a little difficulty, she finally got it poised on the edge of the shelf. To move it farther was beyond Jessie's ability, but she waved Bruce away when he started inching toward her to help.

"I want to do this myself," she told him. "If only to prove that our plan will work."

Rising to a seated position, Jessie planted her feet on the side of the boulder and leaned backward, bracing herself with her hands on the raw ground behind her. She inched forward a bit, raising her knees, then shoved with both feet to send the boulder off the mesa's edge.

For what seemed an eternity there was no noise. Then a crashing thud from below and an outburst of yells from the outlaws reached their ears.

"It's working!" Jessie said, turning to Bruce.

She saw Ki then. He was only a few feet away, rolling a huge cylindrical length of stone. The chunk was almost half as large as he was. He looked questioningly at Jessie when he was within a few feet of the edge, and she gestured toward a spot several paces away from the place where her first effort had been made so successfully.

"It's time for me to get busy, because if one big stone's good, three or four more's likely to be better," Bruce remarked, turning and starting back in search of another boulder.

Below Jessie and Ki, the yells of the outlaws began to diminish; then their angry cries were almost drowned out by a fresh scattering of gunfire cracking from their position on the lower mesa. While most of the rifle slugs sailed over the heads of Jessie and Ki, two or three of the bullets raised puffs of dust as they cut through the rim of the mesa inches from Jessie's feet.

Planting her feet in front of herself and shoving, she managed to move backward a few inches while Ki altered his course the slight amount that was needed to place the stone where Jessie had indicated. Even before he had it set in place, Jessie was moving to get into position to send the stone after her first one.

Again she braced her arms on the ground behind her and leaned on them while bending her knees to place her feet against the big chunk of rock. Her first effort moved it only an inch or two, and she worked herself closer to the big chunk of rock to try again. This time she did not object when Ki moved to one end of the stone and Bruce to the other. Their combined efforts got the big rock moving slowly; then it moved more readily, and after a final combined shove from all three of them, it dropped away.

This time the crash of its landing on the lower mesa brought a yowl of pain from the throat of one of the outlaws below as well as the hoarser pulsating whinnies of a horse that has been injured. A moment later a rattling of gunfire began from the outlaws. Most of the slugs sailed above the heads of the three on the ground beside the outlaws' roost, but one or two of them thunked into the roof or upper wall of the hideaway.

"We're hurting them a lot more than they're hurting us," Ki said.

"That's what we set out to do," Jessie reminded him. "And we'll hurt them still more when Bruce gets back with another hunk of stone."

As though he'd been waiting for Jessie's words as a cue, Bruce reached them, rolling a small boulder with each hand as he bent double to avoid drawing more shots from below. "Seeing as how your medicine seems to be working, Jessie, I sorta figured you might like to give that outfit a double dose," he said. "From the way they're yowling like a bunch of bog-holed calves, two of these might be better'n one big one."

"It might at that," Jessie agreed. "Suppose you and Ki pick different places and roll those boulders down yourselves."

Neither of the men hesitated. They pushed the boulders in different directions until a dozen feet or more separated them, then rolled the big stones over the mesa's rim. A silence of a moment or two followed before it was broken by thunks from below and a cacaphony of undecipherable shouts. After a few moments the voices died away.

"They've stopped shooting," Jessie told Ki and Bruce. "And that means they've got to be up to something. We'd better find out what it is."

Before either them could answer or move to stop her, Jessie edged to the rim and planted her palms on the ground, then lifted her head and shoulders to peer down to the lower mesa. No shots greeted her, and she swept the scene below with a half turn of her head before turning back to Ki and Bruce.

"It looks like we've won," she announced. "They're getting on their horses, and that means they're giving up."

Ki and Bruce wasted no time in raising themselves up to look. On the mesa below, the outlaws were loading the sagging body of one of their outfit to drape it across the back of a horse. On another horse was the limp form of another of the horse thieves. The remaining outlaws levered themselves into their saddles and toed their mounts ahead.

★

Chapter 15

None of the three watchers on the mesa's rim spoke for a moment. Then Jessie said, "I'd say we've beaten them pretty badly, but I wonder if their leaving isn't the first move of some kind of trick they've planned?"

"Maybe they've just run short of shells," Bruce suggested.

"That would certainly make sense," Ki agreed. "Because I'm not really sure they've been pushed-on as hard as they might want us to imagine."

Jessie went on, "I think they've got too much of a stake up here to turn and run without trying to get their hands on all that loot they've hidden under the floorboards in the cabin."

"Wouldn't you say that I'd better trail after them a little way, Jessie?" Ki asked. "Just to make sure they're really heading out for good?"

"Not right this minute," Jessie replied. "They'll leave a trail that we can follow without too much trouble. What we'd better do before we start thinking of anything else is tear up the floor of that cabin and collect all their loot we found under it. Bruce, I think you're entitled to every penny of that money, after they wrecked your horse ranch the way they did."

"There's a hundred times more under that floor than it's going to cost me to put my place back together, Jessie," Bruce told her. "And I've got my horse herd back, so—"

"So take the money," Jessie broke in. "We certainly don't want to leave it for the horse thieves."

"But you and Ki—" Bruce began.

Again Jessie interrupted. "I don't need it, and neither does Ki. You do. So take it without arguing any more. Use it to rebuild your house and barn and hire the help you'll need to get started again. Put the rest of it in a bank where you can get out whatever you need to tide you over a bad time, if you should run into one."

"Well, there's a lot more money in that loot than I'm ever going to need," Bruce said. "But some of it could sure come in handy after I get my horses off this mesa here and start building my place up again."

"Good," Jessie said. "If you don't feel like keeping what's left after you do that, I'm sure you'll find somebody who needs at least part of it. You can share it or spend it or save it. I'll leave that up to you."

"Take Jessie's advice, Bruce," Ki suggested. "None of us has any sympathy for the rustlers who got the money by selling stolen horses. They're the most heartless horse thieves we've ever encountered, don't you agree, Jessie?"

"I'm sure there aren't any angels among them," Jessie answered. "Now, we'll go back for some of that loot, then lower Bruce's horses down to the bottom mesa and find a place where we can leave them safely. That'll finish what we have to do here and we'll be free to go after the horse thieves. We've started a job, and I'm not inclined to stop until we finish it."

"My guess from what little sign we've been able to pick up is that we're still on the trail of the horse thieves," Bruce told Jessie and Ki as they finished repacking their saddle gear after a scanty and hurried breakfast.

"Do you think we're gaining any ground on them?" Jessie asked.

"There ain't much of a way we can do that," Bruce frowned. "The trouble is, they know where they're going and we don't. They can push their horses hard, but we got to stop every once in a while and do a lot of crisscrossing to make sure we're still heading right."

"And they'll just keep riding while we're making sure," Ki said and nodded.

"Think a minute, Bruce," Jessie suggested. "You must know this country as well as the horse thieves do. Where would you say they're heading?"

"Maybe I'm wrong, but my first guess is they're figuring to pick up the old army road that leads to what used to be Fort Baker," Bruce said slowly. "For a while it was the only army fort in Nevada Territory, but the soldiers kept getting pulled away, sent to one place or another till after a while there wasn't any more of 'em left. It's just been going to rack and ruin all these years."

"Are there any towns close to it?" Jessie asked.

"Why, that depends on what you call close, Jessie," Bruce replied. "It'd be a two-day ride to any town at all. But from where we are now, I know a shortcut or two that'll get us there maybe just before dark tonight."

"It sounds to me to be the sort of place a gang like the one we're after might be heading for," she said thoughtfully. "It stands to reason that they'd know about the old fort. I'm sure there'd have to be water close to it, and it's not too far from that mesa hideout we've spoiled for them."

"Then let's push on," Ki suggested. "Just before dark would be a good time to attack them."

"We can get there a mite before sunset if we push along pretty good," Bruce said. "Provided that's what you think we need to do, Jessie."

"I certainly can't think of a better idea," she replied. "The faster we wind up this unpleasant job, the better."

• • •

"Another half mile, now, and we'll see the fort," Bruce told Jessie and Ki. "This little gulch we're in opens out and Fort Baker's right on beyond, sorta a hop-skip-jump away."

"If it's that close, we'd better leave the horses here," Ki suggested. "And I'll go ahead to scout, Jessie, if you think it's a good idea to look before we leap."

"Of course it's a good idea." She nodded. "Bruce and I will wait, and if the horse thieves are there, we'll decide when you come back what the best way is to move in on them."

Ki reined away from his companions and toed his horse ahead. He kept the animal at a steady pace between the sheer sides of the gulch until he reached the point where its walls began to slant and the floor grew wider. Furrows started to appear in the crusted sandy bottom. They grew wider and deeper until the sides of the big gully took a sharp downward slant, and before Ki quite realized it, he suddenly found himself in open country.

Ahead he saw a stretch of featureless desert that had only one visible landmark, a crumbling structure of bleached adobe walls, glassless windows, and doorless doorways. A short distance away from one corner of the structure a half-dozen horses were tethered to the chest-high stalks of a dead cholla cactus. Instantly and without taking a second look at the decaying fort, Ki reined his horse around and backtracked to a point where he would not be seen. Then he dropped the reins, knowing the well-trained horse would stand, and returned on foot to a point where, still concealed by the gully's sloping sides, he could inspect the ruined fort.

Motion within what was left of the structure caught Ki's eyes at once. Men were walking around inside what was left of the walls. Ki could glimpse them but not really see them, for the angle from which he was now studying the fort had narrowed the doors and windows to slits and he got only quick passing glimpses of the men inside as they moved around.

Ki did not need to prolong his observation. Only a few moments after he'd begun his watch, one of the men inside the ruins stepped outside the door to sweep the landscape with his eyes and Ki identified him immediately as one of the outlaws from the mesa. That assurance was all Ki needed. He stepped back to his horse and rejoined Jessie and Bruce.

Even before Ki reined in, Jessie called, "Are they the ones we're after?"

"They certainly are," Ki replied. "Five, maybe six from the horses tethered outside. I figure one might be a pack-horse. I didn't want to get too close, so I didn't see all of them. I did get a real clear look at one, and recognized him the minute I saw him."

"Good!" Jessie exclaimed. "Now let's decide how we can capture them as easily and quickly as possible."

She had been looking at the sky. The sun was still hanging above the horizon, but the gully where they'd stopped was already in full shadow. She said, "Another hour or two and it'll be full dark. And I think the easiest plan we can make is none at all. Ki, I suppose the building they're in has windows and doors?"

"Openings, Jessie," Ki replied. "Doorways without doors, windows with no glass in them."

"That makes it easier," Jessie said and nodded. "We'll give them time to fall asleep. I don't suppose they'll have any sort of night guard, but if they do, Ki can go up first and use his *ninjitsu* to quiet the guard, if there is one. Bruce, you and I will be ready to go inside the fort. If there isn't any guard, Ki will go with us, of course. I'll fire one shot through the roof and—"

Ki broke in to say, "There's not any roof, Jessie. But you fire your shot. Bruce and I will be ready to corral the horse thieves. You cover them; we'll tie their hands."

After another moment of silent thought Jessie went on, "That seems to be all the planning we need to do. We can go back up this gully a little way and wait until it's dark.

163

And it might be a good idea for us to nap a little bit. Two of us can sleep while the other one stands watch. Then we'll be fresher than the horse thieves tonight."

Shrouded in darkness, Jessie, Ki, and Bruce stopped at the end of the gully and blinked as they stared at the dim outline of the abandoned fort. The bulk of the building was a dark block against the moonless night sky.

"I think we can be pretty sure they're all asleep by now," Jessie said, her voice just a tone above a whisper. "And since we've been watching we haven't seen any sign of a lookout."

"Why, they likely figure they've got away scot-free, Jessie," Bruce told her. "They've just had things all their own way too long, back at the mesas."

"Then it's time we changed their minds and put them in a place where they'll have to change their ways," Jessie said. "I don't see any reason why we should wait any longer. All of them are certainly asleep by now."

"And all of us know what we'll be doing," Ki put in.

"I'm sure we do," Jessie agreed. "Bruce knows horses better than either of us; it's his job to get them away from that hitch rail so the horse thieves won't have a chance to get away. Ki, you'll go in the back door; I'll go in the front. I'll fire a shot in the air and tell them they're bottled up. I don't intend to do any more shooting than necessary. We want to take them alive and see that they go to a real court trial."

"And I'll stay with *tegatana* as much as I can," Ki said.

"Then let's start," Jessie said. "I'm sure we all feel that we've waited long enough."

Moving carefully, their feet making only whispers of noise as they crossed the sandy soil, they walked to the derelict fort. None of them spoke. Bruce headed for the tethered horses and Ki started around the building, while Jessie stopped at the doorless front door. Snores and puffs of deep breathing were all she heard.

Peering carefully inside, she could see the blanket-covered

164

forms of the five sleeping horse thieves, dark rectangles on the floor only vaguely visible in the gloom. Raising her rifle, Jessie waited until her judgment told her that Ki and Bruce had been allowed enough time to get into position. She selected an open stretch of floor between two of the recumbent forms and triggered off a shot, the crack of the rifle sounding like a small cannon in the night's stillness.

Only a second or two passed before the sleeping men were tossing their blankets off and getting to their feet, their curses and shouts of surprise a babble of undistinguishable voices in the darkness. Before the horse thieves could shake off the shock of their rude awakening, Jessie let off a second shot, which sang across the width of the cabin and buried itself in the earthen wall.

"You men are covered from every side!" Jessie called. "Don't pick up a gun or even try to! It's worth your life if you do!"

She saw the glistening streak of blued steel as a faint streak in the darkness and started to swing the muzzle of her rifle in the direction of the man who'd raised his weapon, but the glinting steel of Ki's *shuriken* buried itself in the outlaw's arm before he could swing the rifle around. The gun clattered to the floor as a yell of pain broke from his lips.

From the corner of her eyes Jessie saw that one of the men who still hadn't managed to get to his feet was bringing up his revolver. Jessie swung her Winchester to cover him as he was still raising the weapon and shot the gun out of his hand. His yowl was not quite loud enough to drown the noise made by the pistol as it hit the floor after being torn from his hand.

"That's enough!" one of the outlaws shouted. "Give up, fellows! Toss down your guns or we'll all wind up dead!"

None of the outlaws spoke, but the metallic thunking of a pistol sounded as one weapon hit the floor. A final thud broke the momentary silence when the remaining outlaw let his weapon drop as well.

"All right!" one of them called. "You got us! We give up! Just don't turn us over to no lynch mob when you take us in!"

"Don't worry," Jessie assured them, raising her voice to make sure she was heard over the babble. "We'll see that you get a court trial and a sentence from a real judge before you go to the gallows for murder and horse stealing. Now, stand with your faces to the wall, and put your hands behind you so we can tie you up. Then, we'll deliver you to the nearest sheriff, and after that . . . well, you know as well as I do what's going to happen to you."

"Home certainly does look good, doesn't it, Ki?" Jessie asked as they topped the last rise on the Circle Star's rolling range and the main house and other buildings came into sight.

"It looks a lot better than the desert country," Ki agreed. "And the little roan that Bruce is saving for you ought to turn out to be a right biddable piece of horseflesh."

"Oh, I'm sure he will be," Jessie agreed. "But there never was and never will be a horse like Sun. And he—"

Jessie broke off as she saw the magnificent palomino emerge from the barn, tossing its head as it began galloping toward them. She sat silent, watching Sun as he came closer. Then she turned to Ki.

"I hope you won't mind if I gallop ahead of you, Ki. I'm going to go meet Sun and ride him the rest of the way to the main house. That's the only thing Sun and I both need to be sure that I'm home again where both of us belong."

Book One
(1864–1867)

It is my unhappy lot to write the closing entry in this journal.

Clay Halser is dead, killed this morning in my presence.

I have known him since we met during the latter days of The War Between The States. I have run across him, on occasion, through ensuing years and am, in fact, partially responsible (albeit involuntarily) for a portion of the legend which has magnified around him.

It is for these reasons (and another more important) that I make this final entry.

I am in Silver Gulch acquiring research matter toward the preparation of a volume on the history of this territory (Colorado), which has recently become the thirty-eighth state of our Union.

I was having breakfast in the dining room of the *Silver Lode Hotel* when a man entered and sat down at a table across the room, his back to the wall. Initially, I failed to recognize him though there was, in his comportment, something familiar.

Several minutes later (to my startlement), I realized that

it was none other than Clay Halser. True, I had not laid eyes on him for many years. Nonetheless, I was completely taken back by the change in his appearance.

I was not, at that point, aware of his age, but took it to be somewhere in the middle thirties. Contrary to this, he presented the aspect of a man at least a decade older.

His face was haggard, his complexion (in my memory, quite ruddy) pale to the point of being ashen. His eyes, formerly suffused with animation, now looked burned out, dead. What many horrific sights those eyes had beheld I could not—and cannot—begin to estimate. Whatever those sights, however, no evidence of them had been reflected in his eyes before; it was as though he'd been emotionally immune.

He was no longer so. Rather, one could easily imagine that his eyes were gazing, in that very moment, at those bloody sights, dredging from the depths within his mind to which he'd relegated them, all their awful measure.

From the standpoint of physique, his deterioration was equally marked. I had always known him as a man of vigorous health, a condition necessary to sustain him in the execution of his harrowing duties. He was not a tall man; I would gauge his height at five feet ten inches maximum, perhaps an inch or so less, since his upright carriage and customary dress of black suit, hat, and boots might have afforded him the look of standing taller than he did. He had always been extremely well-presented though, with a broad chest, narrow waist, and pantherlike grace of movement; all in all, a picture of vitality.

Now, as he ate his meal across from me, I felt as though, by some bizarre transfiguration, I was gazing at an old man.

He had lost considerable weight and his dark suit (it, too, seemed worn and past its time) hung loosely on his frame. To my further disquiet, I noted a threading of gray through his dark blonde hair and saw a tremor in his hands completely foreign to the young man I had known.

172

I came close to summary departure. To my shame, I nearly chose to leave rather than accost him. Despite the congenial relationship I had enjoyed with him throughout the past decade, I found myself so totally dismayed by the alteration in his looks that I lacked the will to rise and cross the room to him, preferring to consider hasty exit. (I discovered, later, that the reason he had failed to notice me was that his vision, always so acute before, was now inordinately weak.)

At last, however, girding up my will, I stood and moved across the dining room, attempting to fix a smile of pleased surprise on my lips and hoping he would not be too aware of my distress.

"Well, good morning, Clay," I said, as evenly as possible.

I came close to baring my deception at the outset for, as he looked up sharply at me, his expression one of taut alarm, a perceptible "tic" under his right eye, I was hard put not to draw back apprehensively.

Abruptly, then, he smiled (though it was more a ghost of the smile I remembered). "*Frank,*" he said and jumped to his feet. No, that is not an accurate description of his movement. It may well have been his intent to jump up and welcome me with avid handshake. As it happened, his stand was labored, his hand grip lacking in strength. "How *are* you?" he inquired. "It is good to see you."

"I'm fine," I answered.

"Good." He nodded, gesturing toward the table. "Join me."

I hope my momentary hesitation passed his notice. "I'd be happy to," I told him.

"Good," he said again.

We each sat down, he with his back toward the wall again. As we did, I noted how his gaunt frame slumped into the chair, so different from the movement of his earlier days.

He asked me if I'd eaten breakfast.

"Yes." I pointed across the room. "I was finishing when you entered."

"I am glad you came over," he said.

There was a momentary silence. Uncomfortable, I tried to think of something to say.

He helped me out. (I wonder, now, if it was deliberate; if he had, already, taken note of my discomfort.) "Well, old fellow," he asked, "what brings you to this neck of the woods?"

I explained my presence in Silver Gulch and, as I did, being now so close to him, was able to distinguish, in detail, the astounding metamorphosis which time (and experience) had effected.

There seemed to be, indelibly impressed on his still handsome face, a look of unutterable sorrow. His former blitheness had completely vanished and it was oppressive to behold what had occurred to his expression, to see the palsied gestures of his hands as he spoke, perceive the constant shifting of his eyes as though he was anticipating that, at any second, some impending danger might be thrust upon him.

I tried to coerce myself not to observe these things, concentrating on the task of bringing him "up to date" on my activities since last we'd met; no match for his activities, God knows.

"What about you?" I finally asked; I had no more to say about myself. "What are you doing these days?"

"Oh, gambling," he said, his listless tone indicative of his regard for that pursuit.

"No marshaling anymore?" I asked.

He shook his head. "Strictly the circuit," he answered.

"Circuit?" I wasn't really curious but feared the onset of silence and spoke the first word that occurred to me.

"A league of boomtown havens for faro players," he replied. "South Texas up to South Dakota—Idaho to Arizona. There is money to be gotten everywhere. Not that I am good enough to make a raise. And not that it's important if I do, at any rate. I only gamble for something to do."

All the time he spoke, his eyes kept shifting, searching; was it *waiting*?

As silence threatened once again, I quickly spoke. "Well, you have traveled quite a long road since the War," I said. "A long, exciting road." I forced a smile. "*Adventurous,*" I added.

His answering smile was as sadly bitter and exhausted as any I have ever witnessed. "Yes, the writers of the stories have made it all sound very colorful," he said. He leaned back with a heavy sigh, regarding me. "I even thought it so myself at one time. Now I recognize it all for what it was." There was a tightening around his eyes. "Frank, it was drab, and dirty, and there was a lot of blood."

I had no idea how to respond to that and, in spite of my resolve, let silence fall between us once more.

Silence broke in a way that made my flesh go cold. A young man's voice behind me, from some distance in the room. "So that is him," the voice said loudly. "Well, he does not look like much to me."

I'd begun to turn when Clay reached out and gripped my arm. "Don't bother looking," he instructed me. "It's best to ignore them. I have found the more attention paid, the more difficult they are to shake in the long run."

He smiled but there was little humor in it. "Don't be concerned," he said. "It happens all the time. They spout a while, then go away, and brag that Halser took their guff and never did a thing. It makes them feel important. I don't mind. I've grown accustomed to it."

At which point, the boy—I could now tell, from the timbre of his voice, that he had not attained his majority—spoke again.

"He looks like nothing at all to me to be so all-fired famous a fighter with his guns," he said.

I confess the hostile quaver of his voice unsettled me. Seeing my reaction, Clay smiled and was about to speak when the boy—perhaps seeing the smile and angered by it—added, in a tone resounding enough to be heard in the lobby, "In fact, I believe he looks like a woman-hearted coward, that is what he looks like to me!"

"Don't worry now," Clay reassured me. "He'll blow himself out of steam presently and crawl away." I felt some sense of relief to see a glimmer of the old sauce in his eyes. "Probably to visit, with uncommon haste, the nearest outhouse."

Still, the boy kept on with stubborn malice. "My name is Billy Howard," he announced. "And I am going to make . . ."

He went abruptly mute as Clay unbuttoned his dark frock coat to reveal a butt-reversed Colt at his left side. It was little wonder. Even I, a friend of Clay's, felt a chill of premonition at the movement. What spasm of dread it must have caused in the boy's heart, I can scarcely imagine.

"Sometimes I have to go this far," Clay told me. "Usually I wait longer but, since you are with me . . ." He let the sentence go unfinished and lifted his cup again.

I wanted to believe the incident was closed but, as we spoke—me asking questions to distract my mind from its foreboding state—I seemed to feel the presence of the boy behind me like some constant wraith.

"How are all your friends?" I asked.

"Dead," Clay answered.

"*All* of them?"

He nodded. "Yes. Jim Clements. Ben Pickett. John Harris." I saw a movement in his throat. "Henry Blackstone. All of them."

I had some difficulty breathing. I kept expecting to hear the boy's voice again. "What about your wife?" I asked.

"I have not heard from her in some time," he replied. "We are estranged."

"How old is your daughter now?"

"Three in January," he answered, his look of sadness deepening. I regretted having asked and quickly said, "What about your family in Indiana?"

"I went back to visit them last year," he said. "It was a waste."

I did not want to know, but heard myself inquiring nonetheless, "Why?"

"Oh . . . what I have become," he said. "What journalists have made me. Not you," he amended, believing, I suppose, that he'd insulted me. "My reputation, I mean. It stood like a wall between my family and me. I don't think they saw me. Not *me*. They saw what they believed I am."

The voice of Billy Howard made me start. "Well, why does he just *sit* there?" he said.

Clay ignored him. Or, perhaps, he did not even hear, so deep was he immersed in black thoughts.

"Hickok was right," he said, "I am not a man anymore. I'm a figment of imagination. Do you know, I looked at my reflection in the mirror this morning and did not even know who I was looking at? Who is that staring at me? I wondered. Clay Halser of Pine Grove? Or the *Hero of The Plains?*" he finished with contempt.

"*Well?*" demanded Billy Howard. "Why *does* he?"

Clay was silent for a passage of seconds and I felt my muscles drawing in, anticipating God knew what.

"I had no answer for my mirror," he went on then. "I have no answers left for anyone. All I know is that I am tired. They have offered me the job of City Marshal here and, although I could use the money, I cannot find it in myself to accept."

Clay Halser stared into my eyes and told me quietly, "To answer your long-time question: yes, Frank, I have learned what fear is. Though not fear of . . ."

He broke off as the boy spoke again, his tone now venomous. "I think he is afraid of me," said Billy Howard.

Clay drew in a long, deep breath, then slowly shifted his gaze to look across my shoulder. I sat immobile, conscious of an air of tension in the entire room now, everyone waiting with held breath.

"That is what I think," the boy's voice said. "I think Almighty God Halser is afraid of me."

Clay said nothing, looking past me at the boy. I did not dare to turn. I sat there, petrified.

"I think the Almighty God Halser is a yellow skunk!" cried Billy Howard. "I think he is a murderer who shoots men in the back and will not . . . !"

The boy's voice stopped again as Clay stood so abruptly that I felt a painful jolting in my heart. "I'll be right back," he said.

He walked past me and, shuddering, I turned to watch. It had grown so deathly still in the room that, as I did, the legs of my chair squeaked and caused some nearby diners to start.

I saw, now, for the first time, Clay Halser's challenger and was aghast at the callow look of him. He could not have been more than sixteen years of age and might well have been younger, his face speckled with skin blemishes, his dark hair long and shaggy. He was poorly dressed and had an old six-shooter pushed beneath the waistband of his faded trousers.

I wondered vaguely whether I should move, for I was sitting in whatever line of fire the boy might direct. I wondered vaguely if the other diners were wondering the same thing. If they were, their limbs were as frozen as mine.

I heard every word exchanged by the two.

"Now don't you think that we have had enough of this?" Clay said to the boy. "These folks are having their breakfast and I think that we should let them eat their meal in peace."

"Step out into the street then," said the boy.

"Now why should I step out into the street?" Clay asked. I knew it was no question. He was doing what he could to calm the agitated boy—that agitation obvious as the boy replied, "To fight me with your gun."

"You don't want to fight me," Clay informed him. "You would just be killed and no one would be better for it."

"You mean *you* don't want to fight *me*," the youth retorted. Even from where I sat, I could see that his face was almost white; it was clear that he was terror-stricken.

Still, he would not allow himself to back off, though Clay was giving him full opportunity. "*You* don't want to fight *me*," he repeated.

"That is not the case at all," Clay replied. "It is just that I am tired of fighting."

"I *thought* so!" cried the boy with malignant glee.

"Look," Clay told him quietly, "if it will make you feel good, you are free to tell your friends, or anyone you choose, that I backed down from you. You have my permission to do that."

"I don't need your d——d permission," snarled the boy. With a sudden move, he scraped his chair back, rising to his feet. Unnervingly, he seemed to be gaining resolution rather than losing it—as though, in some way, he sensed the weakness in Clay, despite the fact that Clay was famous for his prowess with the handgun. "I am sick of listening to you," he declared. "Are you going to step outside with me and pull your gun like a man, or do I shoot you down like a dog?"

"Go *home*, boy," Clay responded—and I felt an icy grip of premonition strike me full force as his voice broke in the middle of a word.

"Pull, you yellow b——d," Billy Howard ordered him.

Several diners close to them lunged up from their tables, scattering for the lobby. Clay stood motionless.

"I said *pull*, you God d——d son of a b——h!" Billy Howard shouted.

"No," was all Clay Halser answered.

"Then *I* will!" cried the boy.

Before his gun was halfway from the waistband of his trousers, Clay's had cleared its holster. Then—with what capricious twist of fate!—his shot misfired and, before he could squeeze off another, the boy's gun had discharged and a bullet struck Clay full in the chest, sending him reeling back to hit a table, then sprawl sideways to the floor.

Through the pall of dark smoke, Billy Howard gaped down at his victim. "I did it," he muttered. "I *did* it." Though chance alone had done it.

Suddenly, his pistol clattered to the floor as his fingers lost their holding power and, with a cry of what he likely thought was victory, he bolted from the room. (Later, I heard, he was killed in a knife fight over a poker game somewhere near Bijou Basin.)

By then, I'd reached Clay, who had rolled onto his back, a dazed expression on his face, his right hand pressed against the blood-pumping wound in the center of his chest. I shouted for someone to get a doctor, and saw some man go dashing toward the lobby. Clay attempted to sit up, but did not have the strength, and slumped back.

Hastily, I knelt beside him and removed my coat to form a pillow underneath his head, then wedged my handkerchief between his fingers and the wound. As I did, he looked at me as though I were a stranger. Finally, he blinked and, to my startlement, began to chuckle. "The one time I di . . ." I could not make out the rest. "What, Clay?" I asked distractedly, wondering if I should try to stop the bleeding in some other way.

He chuckled again. "The one day I did not reload," he repeated with effort. "Ben would laugh at that."

He swallowed, then began to make a choking noise, a trickle of blood issuing from the left-hand corner of his mouth. "Hang on," I said, pressing my hand to his shoulder. "The doctor will be here directly."

He shook his head with several hitching movements. "No sawbones can remove me from *this* tight," he said.

He stared up at the ceiling now, his breath a liquid sound that made me shiver. I did not know what to say, but could only keep directing worried (and increasingly angry) glances toward the lobby. "Where *is* he?" I muttered.

180

Clay made a ghastly, wheezing noise, then said, "My God." His fingers closed in, clutching at the already blood-soaked handkerchief. "I am going to die." Another strangling breath. "And I am only thirty-one years old."

Instant tears distorted my vision. *Thirty-one?*

Clay murmured something I could not hear. Automatically, I bent over and he repeated, in a labored whisper, "She was such a pretty girl."

"Who?" I asked; could not help but ask.

"Mary Jane," he answered. He could barely speak by then. Straightening up, I saw the grayness of death seeping into his face and knew that there were only moments left to him.

He made a sound which might have been a chuckle had it not emerged in such a hideously bubbling manner. His eyes seemed lit now with some kind of strange amusement. "I could have married her," he managed to say. "I could still be there." He stared into his fading thoughts. "Then I would never have . . ."

At which his stare went lifeless and he expired.

I gazed at him until the doctor came. Then the two of us lifted his body—how *frail* it was—and placed it on a nearby table. The doctor closed Clay's eyes and I crossed Clay's arms on his chest after buttoning his coat across the ugly wound. Now he looked almost at peace, his expression that of a sleeping boy.

Soon people began to enter the dining room. In a short while, everyone in Silver Gulch, it seemed, had heard about Clay's death and come running to view the remains. They shuffled past his impromptu bier in a double line, gazed at him and, ofttimes, murmured some remark about his life and death.

As I stood beside the table, looking at the gray, still features, I wondered what Clay had been about to say before the rancorous voice of Billy Howard had interrupted. He'd said that he had learned what fear is, "though not fear of . . ." What words had he been about to say? Though not fear of other men? Of danger? Of death?

181

Later on, the undertaker came and took Clay's body after I had guaranteed his payment. That done, I was requested, by the manager of the hotel, to examine Clay's room and see to the disposal of his meager goods. This I did and will return his possessions to his family in Indiana.

With one exception.

In a lower bureau drawer, I found a stack of Record Books bound together with heavy twine. They turned out to be a journal which Clay Halser kept from the latter part of the War to this very morning.

It is my conviction that these books deserve to be published. Not in their entirety, of course; if that were done, I estimate the book would run in excess of a thousand pages. Moreover, there are many entries which, while perhaps of interest to immediate family (who will, of course, receive the Record Books when I have finished partially transcribing them), contribute nothing to the main thrust of his account, which is the unfoldment of his life as a nationally recognized lawman and gunfighter.

Accordingly, I plan to eliminate those sections of the journal which chronicle that variety of events which any man might experience during twelve years' time. After all, as hair-raising as Clay's life was, he could not possibly exist on the razor edge of peril every day of his life. As proof of this, I will incorporate a random sampling of those entries which may be considered, from a "thrilling" standpoint, more mundane.

In this way—concentrating on the sequences of "action"— it is hoped that the general reader, who might otherwise ignore the narrative because of its unwieldy length, will more willingly expose his interest to the life of one whom another journalist has referred to as "The Prince of Pistoleers."

Toward this end, I will, additionally, attempt to make corrections in the spelling, grammar and, especially, punctuation of the journal, leaving, as an indication of this necessity, the opening entry. It goes without saying that subsequent entries need less attention to this aspect since Clay

Halser learned, by various means, to read and write with more skill in his later years.

I hope the reader will concur that, while there might well be a certain charm in viewing the entries precisely as Clay Halser wrote them, the difficulty in following his style through virtually an entire book would make the reading far too difficult. It is for this reason that I have tried to simplify his phraseology without—I trust—sacrificing the basic flavor of his language.

Keep in mind, then, that if the chronology of this account is, now and then, sporadic (with occasional truncated entries), it is because I have used, as its main basis, Clay Halser's life as a man of violence. I hope, by doing this, that I will not unbalance the impression of his personality. While trying not to intrude unduly on the texture of the journal, I may occasionally break into it if I believe my observations may enable the reader to better understand the protagonist of what is probably the bloodiest sequence of events to ever take place on the American frontier.

I plan to do all this, not for personal encomiums, but because I hope that I may be the agency by which the public-at-large may come to know Clay Halser's singular story, perhaps to thrill at his exploits, perhaps to moralize but, hopefully, to profit by the reading for, through the page-by-page transition of this man from high-hearted exuberance to hopeless resignation, we may, perhaps, achieve some insight into a sad, albeit fascinating and exciting, phenomenon of our times.

Frank Leslie
April 19, 1876